By the book.

"This is a piece of cake," I said. "With that subpoena, I just get to pretend that I'm part of the summer education program they run at the DA's office."

"What will you do with the book?"

"The lab that does all the city's DNA work for the police department is at the Office of the Chief Medical Examiner. I've been there dozens of times with my mother. The head of the lab actually came to Ditchley with me to show the biology class how DNA is extracted from evidence and used to solve crimes. I've got lots of buddies at the lab."

Liza couldn't even look me in the eye.

"All we have to do is put the book in a large brown supermarket shopping bag—never put evidence in plastic—and we take it to the lab. We'll get it jumped to the front of the line for examination. C'mon."

Liza didn't budge.

"What's the problem?" I asked.

"First of all, we promised your mother and Sam that we wouldn't do anything more about the book thief, okay? That's the most important thing."

OTHER BOOKS YOU MAY ENJOY

THE
DEVLIN
—QUICK—
MYSTERIES

INTO THE LION'S DEN

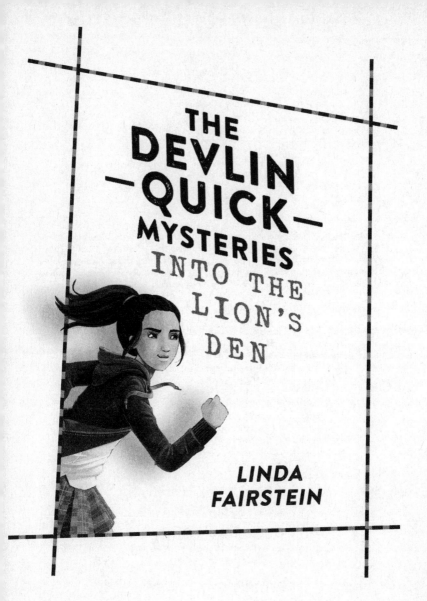

THE
DEVLIN
—QUICK—
MYSTERIES
INTO THE
LION'S
DEN

LINDA
FAIRSTEIN

PUFFIN BOOKS

PUFFIN BOOKS
An imprint of Penguin Random House LLC
375 Hudson Street
New York, New York 10014

First published in the United States of America by Dial Books for Young Readers,
an imprint of Penguin Random House LLC, 2016
Published by Puffin Books, an imprint of Penguin Random House LLC, 2017

THE LIBRARY OF CONGRESS HAS CATALOGED THE DIAL BOOKS FOR YOUNG READERS EDITION AS FOLLOWS:
Names: Fairstein, Linda A., author.
Title: Into the lion's den / Linda Fairstein.
Description: New York, NY : Dial Books for Young Readers, [2016] | Series:
The Devlin Quick mysteries ; 1 | Audience: 8-12. | Summary: "Twelve year
old Devlin Quick is determined to bring a thief to justice when someone
steals a page out of a rare maps book in the New York Public Library"—
Provided by publisher.
Identifiers: LCCN 2016005234| ISBN 9780399186431 (hardcover) |
ISBN 9780399186455 (e-book)
Subjects: | CYAC: Mystery and detective stories. | Maps—Fiction. |
Libraries—Fiction. | New York (N.Y.)—Fiction. | BISAC: JUVENILE FICTION
/ Mysteries & Detective Stories. | JUVENILE FICTION / Action & Adventure /
General. | JUVENILE FICTION / Law & Crime.
Classification: LCC PZ7.1.F346 In 2016 | DDC [Fic]—dc23 LC record available at
https://lccn.loc.gov/2016005234

Puffin Books ISBN 9780399186448

Printed in the United States of America

1 3 5 7 9 10 8 6 4 2

Design by Mina Chung • Text set in Chapparel Pro

For my favorite supersleuths—
Isla, Mila, Eve,
and Sam

1

"I'm trapped!" Liza said.

"What's wrong?" I asked. "I'm worried about you. What's taking you so long?"

"I'm stuck. And I can't exactly talk in here."

I held the phone closer to my ear. "What?"

"Tell me where you are, and I'll meet you in five," she whispered.

"I'm sitting on the lion," I said. "And hurry up because it's really hot outside."

It was three o'clock in the afternoon on a Tuesday in late June. My mother had struck a deal with me at the end of the semester, when my seventh-grade classes finished. If I agreed to take three weeks of summer school courses—not because I needed the credits or anything, but mostly to keep me out of her hair—then I could go on vacation with my best friend's family for three weeks in July.

So far my mother got the better part of the bargain. She usually did. There was a ton of homework that went with the program at the Ditchley School, and Katie's family had changed their summer plans since I signed on to hang out with them. Instead of going to their cool beach house on the ocean in Montauk for the entire two months, Katie's dad got it into his head that bone-dry Big Timber, Montana, was a smart place to buy a ranch just in time for the second half of our school break.

"Get off that lion's back, young lady," the security guard yelled at me from the top of the library steps.

"Okay, sir." I waved at him and slid off the marble statue, jumping from its pedestal to the ground. "No harm, no foul."

Patience and Fortitude, the two stately kings of the jungle, had guarded the entrance to the massive New York Public Library for more than a hundred years. They stood right on Fifth Avenue, in the center of Manhattan, watchdogs over all the action in midtown. I didn't think my wiry frame would have ruffled their manes for the few minutes I had parked myself on top of one of them.

I was dying to call Katie, who had already stationed herself out at the beach until we headed west, to ask what her father, a hedge-fund honcho, suddenly found more appealing about rattlesnakes and mountain lions and black bears in the high desert than swimming and chilling and looking for cute surfers on the East End of Long Island.

"Dev!" Liza was shouting my name as she burst through the front door.

"Glad you unstuck yourself, Liza."

For the moment, I was wrapped up with Liza de Lucena, an Argentinian student who'd gotten a scholarship to the Ditch for the summer and was staying with us as part of the program.

Liza was flying down the staircase like her hair was on fire.

"I was trapped in there," she said. "You don't get it, Dev. It was terrifying."

"Rattlesnakes are terrifying, Liza. This is a library. Worst thing that can happen to you is a bad paper cut."

"You think I'm kidding? It's that man in the navy blue blazer," she said, trying to catch her breath. "The one crossing the street right in front of the bus. I thought if he saw where I was hiding—well, I didn't know what he would do to me."

"Hiding from a librarian?" I asked. The light turned

red as the tall man reached the opposite side of Fifth Avenue. "Look, Liza, they can be tough if you're making noise, but—"

She started to run toward the curb. "You've got to chase him, Dev. You've got to take a picture of him with your phone."

Just what I needed. A drama queen to enliven my summer studies.

"Why me? Is your phone out of juice?"

"Because he saw me, Dev. He knows I watched him take the paper."

I caught up to her at the start of the crosswalk. "He couldn't have taken anything. I told you no one can check things out of this place, Liza. It's not a lending library. It's only for research. It's the most famous research library in the entire world."

"Then he's a thief, Dev. He stole something. You have to take his picture before he gets away."

The word "thief" triggered a hot spot in my brain—there's nothing I like better than a good mystery. I sprinted onto the pavement the second the traffic light switched to green, because Liza had a point. Her pink-and-orange T-shirt had the words NEW YORK plastered across the front. She might as well have been wearing a neon sign that said TOURIST.

The chunky black braid and full set of braces made her a standout among the older bookworms in the reading room.

By the time I crossed the wide avenue, with Liza a few steps behind, the man had turned the corner onto Forty-Second Street.

I had no idea if Liza was right—that he had stolen some kind of paper from the library—but I loved the idea of chasing a possible thief, a person of interest, as my mother would say. I sort of have investigative instincts in my genes, I liked to think. Friends are always coming to me to solve problems, most of which don't take more than simple powers of observation and deduction. A healthy dose of strong nerves is another useful asset, and I seem to have an endless supply of those.

"Excuse me," I said, squeezing between shoppers and sightseers who were hogging the sidewalk, making it impossible for me to get to top speed.

The tall man had long legs and was walking briskly, near the curb to avoid the strolling pedestrians. As nimbly as I could move, I didn't seem to be gaining on him.

I turned to make sure I hadn't lost Liza, who was proving to be a drag on my pace. "He's not carrying anything," I said. "No briefcase, no bag, no paper."

"I saw him cut a page out of a book, Dev. It must have been a rare book, too, because the librarian made him put on white gloves to look at it."

"Cut it?" I kept one eye on the tall man, who was jaywalking in the direction of Grand Central, the huge train terminal that had way too many tracks leading out of town, and dozens of subway entrances that could take him to the far ends of the outer boroughs of the city.

"Yes. He dropped his little knife on the floor and that's what caught my attention. That's when he glared at me. What I saw him doing can't be legal, can it?"

Now I shifted into high gear. The yellow caution light was about to switch to red, but I ran into the crosswalk and made it to the north side of Forty-Second Street, certain that a crime had been committed.

"Wait up, Dev!" I could hear Liza shouting from the farside of a city bus.

There was no point waiting for her. Maybe the meek will inherit the earth, but they're not likely to get Manhattan in that deal. And they sure won't catch any bad guys. I was pumped up by a new fact:

She had seen a sharp blade dissecting the pages of a rare book. That sounded like a really serious crime—maybe even a felony.

The tall man turned into the corner doorway of the vast train terminal.

Could be my lucky day. The way into Grand Central at that point happened to be a really long ramp—not a single step in sight—that led from the sidewalk down a slope into the very middle of the main floor. It was straight downhill from here.

I had my cell phone in my left hand, punching up the camera icon as I skirted all the commuters and tourists who were clogging the corridors of the terminal.

I saw the solution to my problem directly in my path. Three boys, younger than me, were studying a subway map, each holding a skateboard under his arm as they argued over directions.

"I'll give it back to you in five," I said, pulling the board away from the shortest one. "Meet you at the information booth."

I put the board on the ground and stepped on it with my left foot, pushing off in pursuit of my long-legged adversary.

The boys shouted after me and gave chase. Good

thing it wasn't rush hour or I might have run over some tired feet. As it was, I got yelled at by stragglers of all shapes and sizes as I weaved a path around and through them. I didn't understand why they couldn't see me coming and just step aside.

I was nipping at the tall man's heels when he made a sudden turn to the left as he reached the bottom of the ramp.

I tried to bail from the board, but it bucked and tossed me onto the marble floor.

The kid whose board I had borrowed was almost on me. That was when he let out a loud cry: "Stop, thief!"

The tall man's head snapped around while the three boys charged directly at me. I was flat on my back but I scrambled onto my knees, lifted my hand, and snapped a few photos of him.

A small crowd was gathering around *me*—instead of the real thief—as I got to my feet. The boy had retrieved his board and was running to catch up with his pals without waiting for my apology or explanation, so people walked away.

Liza was running down the ramp, well-meaning I'm sure, but too late to be useful. "Did you lose him?"

I shook my head as I saw the suspect passing

through the wrought-iron gates at Track 113, just before the conductor slammed them shut.

"Open up, please, sir!" I called to him as he also walked toward the train.

"Too late, young lady. Where are you going?"

I stepped back to see the stops on the large schedule posted next to the gate, but the conductor just kept on walking.

"I'm—I'm . . . going to . . . ," I said, skimming the names of the familiar Westchester County towns from top to bottom before settling on a destination farther north. "I'm going to Poughkeepsie."

"End of the line, is it?" he said, turning to point to his right. "Track 102 in forty-five minutes. This train has already left the station."

2

"You're bleeding, Dev," Liza said.

She was sitting next to me in the last car of the 4 train, which is the Lexington Avenue Express. The Ditch uniform skirt was absurdly short, and my exposed knees were scraped and bloody. I dabbed at them with a napkin left over from our stop at the Shake Shack for a post-pursuit snack.

"I'm so bummed that we missed him," I said.

"Me, too."

Liza's English was almost unaccented and practically perfect. In just our short time together, it was pretty clear that even our colloquialisms were familiar to kids at the American School in Buenos Aires.

"Beyond bummed," I said, punching up the photos I took of the thief.

"May I see those?"

"Not my best work, Liza," I said, holding out my phone.

The images I shot from my position on the floor of Grand Central's main concourse were mostly blurry. The subject of my investigation appeared to be looming over me—quite out of proportion because I hadn't really gotten all up in his face. The angle captured the smooth lines of his chin from below, his flared nostrils, the tip of his nose, and the rim of his tortoiseshell glasses. It wouldn't make for a proper WANTED poster.

"That's him," Liza said. "That's the guy. What are we going to do now?"

"I'd like to get some professional help."

"We should have gone back to the library."

"Oh, we're going to do that, for sure," I said. "But I want them to take us seriously when we go there. I want to make sure there are forensics to back us up."

"Forensics? Good idea, Dev. But where do we go for that? Will one of the teachers be able to help us with it?"

"Better than that, Liza. The New York Police Department has an amazing range of new techniques to catch criminals."

"I don't even know what the man stole," Liza

said. I could hear her gulp as she tried to backstep. "You think the police will get involved in a case like this?"

"Count on it."

"In my country, I don't believe the officials would take kids like us seriously, especially about a matter like this, with no grown-up witnesses."

"Zero tolerance here in New York, Liza. Quality of life crimes and all that. You can't have people stealing from our great public institutions." I was beginning to sound more like my grandmother than my grandmother did.

The subway car was rocking back and forth. There was only one stop between Grand Central and the Brooklyn Bridge station, and the express train could make the trip in fourteen minutes.

I turned on my phone and started texting.

"Who are you talking to?" Liza asked.

"I have to tell my friend Katie what's going on. She might not appreciate us working this case without her," I said. "And then I need to make sure the detective I want to meet with is in his office."

"How about Natasha? Isn't she expecting us at the apartment?"

"I'll tell her next. She'll be totally on board with it. She knows my mother is coming home from her business trip tonight."

Natasha has been living with us for years and was like a big sister to me. Now that I was twelve, I didn't need a babysitter anymore, but I knew she was always watching out for me and she helped out my mom by cooking dinner most nights, too.

"If you're sure that's okay," Liza said.

Liza still hadn't met my mother, who'd been in Washington, DC, since Sunday afternoon. While I was texting, Liza opened her backpack and took out a book. It was one of those Brontë sisters' novels, not that I could ever keep anything those three girls wrote straight.

"Subway rules, Liza. No reading on the train." Liza had only arrived in New York on Sunday evening—the night before last. Ditchley was a short walk from my apartment, so she didn't have any knowledge of public transportation.

"What are you talking about? It's a perfectly good time to read."

"Not in my experience," I said. "You can't bury your nose in a book. A lot of stuff goes down on the subway. You have to be alert and take it all in."

She sighed and closed the book. "What are the other rules?"

"Never look at a map while you're sitting on a train."

"But this is only my second time on the subway. From school to the library, and now this. One day I'm going to have to go somewhere without you, and I'll have to use one."

"Oh, boy. That would really make you a sitting duck," I said, shaking my head. "Plan your route at home—study the map on the kitchen table before you get on the train. Otherwise someone will target you as an out-of-towner and try to take advantage of you."

"But—"

"You saw how I gamed that kid right out of his skateboard, didn't you?"

I could see I was freaking her out. "I'll write you the list of subway rules," I said, standing up and grabbing the pole as the train slowed down, headed into the station. "C'mon. This is our stop."

We climbed the steps out of the subway and emerged in the middle of Foley Square, with all the courthouses around us. Liza followed me to the right, past the line of food trucks and behind the massive granite facade of the federal court.

The modern building ahead of us was bright redbrick, fifteen stories tall, overlooking the East River. There was a guardhouse thirty feet from the entrance, and we stopped there to show our student IDs to the uniformed officer.

"Sergeant Tapply is expecting us," I said. "I'm Devlin Quick. He should have added us a few minutes ago."

"Okay, Miss Quick. He just called your names down to us," the officer said, checking the visitors' list on his clipboard. "You need to empty your pockets and put that backpack through the metal detector inside. Then take the elevator to fourteen."

"There are police everywhere," Liza said.

Men and women in blue uniforms were coming and going from the building like a steady swarm of ants. The men in suits were undoubtedly from the detective bureau.

I pointed to the huge letters on the wall next to the front door. "One Police Plaza," I said. "It's headquarters for all of New York City."

More cops were inside the door to guide us through the security process. Several nodded at me as we passed through the lobby and turned into the elevator bank. I didn't want Liza to think I was showing off, so I didn't say anything to anyone.

I pressed the button for the fourteenth floor. The signage everywhere in the elevator and on the walls said ONE PP.

"PP," Liza repeated to herself. "Police Plaza."

"Yeah, this is where all the good stuff happens, Liza. This is where the major cases are solved," I said. "That's why the cops claim that 'PP' really stands for the 'Puzzle Palace.'"

We walked down a long corridor, and I stopped in front of a glass door with large gold lettering on it.

POLICE COMMISSIONER was printed across the top, and on the bottom were the words CITY OF NEW YORK.

In the very middle of the glass panel was my mother's name, in bold gold paint outlined in black: BLAINE QUICK.

Liza grabbed my arm and read the name out loud. "That's your mother?"

"Pretty awesome, isn't it? She's the police commissioner of New York City."

3

"Speak of the devil and she will indeed appear," Andrew Tapply said, getting up from behind his desk to high-five me. "The devil Quick herself."

"Hey, Tapp. Thanks for letting us in," I said. "This is my friend, Liza de Lucena."

Liza had broken into a sweat. The idea of being in the commissioner's office seemed to overwhelm her more than a chase through midtown streets.

"Good to meet you, Liza. I know all about you," Tapp said, flashing a welcoming grin. "I'm the guy that ran the background check on your family."

Liza seemed startled. "All the school told my family is that your mother was a city official. We had no idea what her position was."

I bit my lip and shook my head.

"Nothing personal, you understand. It's routine

for anyone coming to stay in the commissioner's apartment."

"It's why nobody except Katie wants to do sleepovers with me," I said, glancing at Liza.

"Your mother's not here, Dev," Tapp said.

"I know. She's been away at a two-day meeting with Homeland Security in DC. Liza hasn't even met her yet," I said. "She'll be home in time to have dinner with us tonight."

"Did you bring Liza down to show her around the office?" Tapp asked, opening the door to my mother's suite, with its spectacular view of the Brooklyn Bridge and most of New York Harbor. "You're welcome to it."

But Liza was more interested in the trappings that came with the commissioner's job than in the view. There was the large photograph of my mother that hung on the wall and in every station house in the city, the American flag flanked by the New York City colors, and the NYPD banner, too, along with pictures of Mom with all the dignitaries who passed through town on her watch. Liza ran her hand over the leather inlay on top of the enormous desk.

"Sit down at her desk, Liza," I said. "Really, you can."

"I'll get you each a soda," Tapp said.

"I also came to pick your brain, Tapp, if you don't mind."

"A little late in the day to try to harvest anything up there, Dev," he said, pointing to the side of his head.

Andy Tapply was the best-natured guy I knew, hand-chosen by my mother to cover her back. He was overweight so he didn't look like everybody's idea of a supercop. But Tapp had a really big brain and was so trustworthy that he helped guard her post in the palace and oversee her team.

"We've got a class project, Tapp. Summer school at the Ditch. I've got an assignment we need some professional help with, okay?"

"When's the last time I said no to you, Dev? Whatever you need."

I gave him a thumbs-up.

He walked off as Liza pulled the chair out and sat down, ogling all the objects and memorabilia in front of her.

"Do you know who Teddy Roosevelt was?" I asked. "He was our—"

"Of course I do. He was your twenty-sixth president, and he also came to South America to explore the River of Doubt," Liza said. "You've got to get over this idea that you think you're the only one who knows anything, Dev."

That was another one of my faults, as my mother frequently reminded me.

"Sorry. I didn't imagine you'd have any reason to learn he had once been the police commissioner of New York City, in 1895," I said. "That's actually TR's desk that you're leaning on. For real."

Liza sat up straight in the chair and lifted her arms off the desk, like it might shock her.

"It's okay. We're allowed to be here."

"But what did you tell the sergeant?" Liza asked. "Is the school project you're talking about actually the library thief?"

"Sort of. Tapp will be cool with that."

"But it's a lie, Dev."

I turned to the window and rolled my eyes. "No, it's not what you think, Liza. It's only a fiblet."

"A what? "

"Fiblet" was a word my friends and I used, not likely to be on the agenda at Liza's school.

"Look, Liza," I said, "a lie would be a false statement made with deliberate intent to deceive, right?"

"Exactly. So what's a fiblet?"

"I'm not trying to deceive Tapp, that's for sure," I said. "It's a very innocent exaggeration to enlist his help for what started as your library project for the Ditch. A fiblet is just a harmless misstatement of fact. Can you live with that? Can you please just live with that for today?"

She fidgeted in her chair. "I think what we're doing to try to catch the thief is a very good thing, Dev. I just don't want to get you in trouble with your mother."

"She really values outside-the-box thinking, Liza. She's going to love it when I tell her how brave you were to call out that man."

Tapp came back in the room with cold drinks, and he and I seated ourselves opposite Liza. "What's the gig, Dev?"

I leaned in and pulled up my pictures on the cell phone. "So we were at the library this afternoon, working on something for school. Liza thinks she saw—"

"Thinks?" Tapp asked.

"My slip. Liza saw a man slice a page out of a rare book. We'd actually like to catch him, because defacing a book—maybe even a rare one—is a horrible thing to do. That's where I need your help."

"What did the librarian say? Or security? They've got a big force."

"I didn't tell anyone inside," Liza said. "I only told Devlin."

"Look, young lady," Tapp said to me, "you need to march back to the folks in charge and tell them exactly what happened. We got armed robbers and burglars and miscreants of every shape and size to deal with here at headquarters. A single page of literature, Dev? Not exactly my thing."

"Single pages of literature have changed history, Tapp. Think of Harriet Beecher Stowe or Karl Marx or Tom Paine."

"Yeah, those were game changers, all right. But maybe this one was a blank page. Maybe the guy ripped it out of the book because there was nothing on it."

"Don't be silly," I said. "We are going back to the library, of course. Right after class tomorrow. But I thought if you could apply the department's facial recognition software program to my photograph, maybe we could really surprise my mother when she gets home tonight."

Tapp held out his hand to take my phone. "One

thing about Dev's mother, Liza, she's a lady who doesn't take much to surprises. Keep that in mind."

"Yes, sir."

"What do you two know about facial recognition systems?" Tapp asked.

"Nothing," Liza said.

"Only what I've heard Mom talk about," I said. "That it's a computer application to automatically identify a person from a digital image. I think it compares facial features to a database in the department. Like from all the mug shots on file."

"That'll work for starters, Dev," Tapp said. "Law enforcement agencies all over the world have tried to use it, but most of the results have been disappointing. For example, it can be good at full-frontal face photos, with maybe a few degrees off the angle of the shot, but once you get away from that direction, it's not so good. Even a picture of you, with that serious expression on your mug that you got going on right now, won't necessarily match up with a photo taken of you when you're smiling."

He looked down at the photograph for several seconds, then shook his head. "They got a course at your school in photography, Dev? Sign up for it next semester. That's what you need a lesson or two in. Hard to know what we're looking at here."

"It's the man's face all right. It's just that I slipped on the floor of the main concourse at Grand Central and wound up on my back."

"So I'm looking up at a pointy chin, the bottom of the nose of an angry rhino, and a pair of glasses? You can't see anything of his face."

"I would recognize him the minute I saw him again," Liza said.

That's the spirit. Tapp won't want to let you down.

"The first thing we'd need to do is to normalize things to represent the face in a frontal orientation. The tilt or lean of the head here, well, we just won't have anything like that in our system."

"But you'll make a copy of my photo and stick it in your computer, Tapp? Won't you? Just give it a try, running it against thieves known to the department?"

"If that makes you happy, kid, I'll start my day with it tomorrow. Right after the commissioner gives me her permission."

"Here I thought you said you'd do anything for me."

"You've got no official police report, no real

description of the criminal, and no good reason to put my head on the chopping block with my boss. Talk it over with your mother."

"I knew it was a long shot. I just don't want to leave any stone unturned in the investigation," I said. "And I wanted Liza to see the inner sanctum of the Puzzle Palace."

I forwarded the photos to Tapp's e-mail address before standing up.

"Thanks for being so gracious to us," Liza said.

"Next time I'll give you a tour of the whole place— the palace. For now, I'll walk you to the elevator, Dev."

Andrew Tapply gave me a hug, and the doors closed behind us.

"Good try, Dev," Liza said. "That was a really good idea."

"I'm not out of them yet. Good ideas, that is. When we go back to the library after school tomorrow, we can figure out a way to get the perp's DNA off something in the Map Division."

"DNA?" Liza asked. "But there wasn't any blood, thank goodness."

"Yes, but there's likely to be what they call trace evidence in that room where the thief was working."

"What's that?"

"Things he touched, Liza. Particles of DNA come off in the oils that are deposited on surfaces of things."

"He wore cotton gloves, Dev. The librarian gave them to him. Don't you remember I told you that?"

I pursed my lips and had to admit to Liza that I had forgotten that fact in my excitement. But I was an optimist and always ready for a challenge. "The man must have touched something before he put the gloves on—one of those globes or other books or a sign-in register. He didn't walk down Fifth Avenue and into the library wearing white gloves. He's bound to have left some evidence behind."

4

"Mom, is that you?" I took my key out of the lock, pushed the door open, and ran toward the kitchen, where I heard voices.

"Hey, sweetie," she said, opening her arms to embrace me and kiss me on top of my head while our dog rubbed against my legs, wagging her tail furiously. "I've missed you."

"Me too," I said, wrapping my arms around my mother's waist. I could pretend to be as cool as the next guy when I was talking about her, but I couldn't stand going very long without her. We'd been a tight pair all my life.

She reached over my shoulder and extended her hand. "You must be Liza. I'm so sorry I wasn't here to meet you when you arrived, but I'll make up for that during the rest of your stay."

"Thank you so much, Ms. Quick. I'm very grateful

to you for hosting me. It's such an honor to be with you."

"Dev and I are the lucky ones to have you here. It seems like you're enjoying each other's company," she said. "It's almost six thirty. You'll have to tell us all about your long day. Please wash up for dinner, pronto."

"Sam!" I said, turning to face the man leaning against the kitchen counter. "Are you staying for dinner?"

"He's off-duty, Dev," my mother said. "We've been going nonstop for days, so just let him relax."

Sam Cody, the homicide detective who had been assigned to bodyguard my mother a few years ago, switched his cocktail to his left hand and high-fived me with his right.

"Just so long as your mother didn't cook it, I'm in."

The table was set for four of us. "Where's Natasha? I texted her and told her we wouldn't be home until after six. I took Liza to see your office."

"She's gone out with friends. And yes, she told me you'd checked in and would be late. And yes, she walked the dog for you. *Your* dog. She also made a meat loaf for us this afternoon. And mashed potatoes. I'm just heating it up."

"Sam's favorite meal," I said to Liza. "Let's clean up."

We'd been living in our apartment on the Upper East Side since I was five years old. It had three bedrooms—my mother's, the one that Liza was sharing with me, and Natasha's room. I don't even remember what was in there before she came to live with us seven years ago.

I dropped my things on my bed and went into the bathroom. Asta, a very affectionate spaniel terrier mix we rescued from a shelter for my tenth birthday, followed me in. Sam had named her Asta after the dog owned by Nora and Nick Charles, the private detectives in *The Thin Man* books and movies. He liked to tease my mother that her sleuthing was about as professional as Nora Charles's.

"Your mother's so—well, pretty, so soft-looking."

"What were you expecting? Teddy Roosevelt and his mustache?" I started to scrub my face and hands.

"She must have a very tough job, being police commissioner. I was thinking she'd look older and serious," Liza said. "You don't look anything like her."

"I won't take that as an insult, okay? Everyone says that I'm pretty much a carbon copy of my dad. Black hair and green eyes, slender and wiry," I said. "But he died before I was born, so I only know what people tell me, and what he looks like in photographs."

"I'm sorry, I knew your mother was a single mom. I didn't mean to—"

"No reason you should have known anything else." I dried my face on the towel and left the room, closing the bathroom door behind me.

There was a picture of my father on my dresser. He was a very handsome man—dashing, my grandmother always said—and very kind, according to everyone who knew him. His name was Devlin, too. Every time I looked at his face I tried to imagine what he would have been like in my life.

And every day there were two things I tried to do to live up to his name. One was to take care of my mother as best as I could. Fortunately there were people like Natasha and Sam and Tapp, as well as all her friends, to help me with that. The other was to do things that I thought would have made him proud to have me as a daughter.

"Let's go, girls," my mother called out. "Everything's hot."

Liza followed me down the hall to the table in our kitchen. There was an actual dining room in the apartment, but it had been turned into my mother's home office years ago, with one corner of the table open so I could keep my laptop there when she was working. It was swamped with her papers, case reports, mayoral directives, and printed-out e-mails from every law enforcement agency in the country.

My mother was pouring wine for Sam and for herself. I reached into the refrigerator for a bottle of milk when she served up the dinner plates.

"Tell us about your first impressions of New York, Liza," she said. "How do you like it?"

"It's fascinating, Ms. Quick," Liza said. She was happy and animated and eager to answer all the questions my mother asked. They talked about school and family and Liza's first two subway rides. "I really think I'm going to like it here."

"What happened at your meeting in DC, Mom?"

"I'm not sure she can tell you without violating protocol, Devlin. Top secret," Sam said, winking at me. He was one of the few people who called me by my full name, and I liked that. "Wait till you get your gold shield. Then we'll see that you get top security clearance."

"How about if we catch a crook? Does that get me the gold?"

"I'd pin it on you myself," Sam said.

"Show it to Liza, will you please?"

Sam took his gold shield out of his pocket and passed it to Liza. It was the coveted prize in the NYPD, the shiny gold badge trimmed with cobalt blue enamel, engraved with the name DETECTIVE SAMUEL CODY and his shield number. He had earned his with brilliant and courageous investigative work.

"No catching crooks, girls. That's what my force is in business to do," my mother said. "Natasha told me your assignment took you to the public library. Sounds interesting. What's that about?"

"You start, Liza," I said, writing the letters DNA on my potatoes with the meat gravy stuck on my knife while I tried to think through how to look for the tall man's genetic fingerprints at the scene of the crime.

"So in our class about world culture, the teacher added a project in which we each have to go to the library, pick one of the famous objects there, and write a paper about it by the end of the summer session."

"You mean you choose a book?"

"No, Ms. Quick. Actually an object from the collections of the library. There are a hundred of them on display now. Like dance cards from nineteenth-century balls and an etching of a turkey that Picasso made. Things that you wouldn't expect a library to own, so not books."

"What are you writing about, Liza?" Sam asked.

"Well, there's a globe in the collection that is one of the rarest in the world. It's made out of copper and it's only five inches around. Nobody knows who made it. It's called the Hunt-Lenox Globe, after the architect who designed a private library for a rich patron named Lenox, but it was created just a little bit after the discovery of the New World."

"Why did you choose it?"

Liza grinned at Sam and her braces glistened. "It was the first representation of the New World known to geographers, and it shows only one continent in the entire Western Hemisphere. Only South America."

"And you think sometimes we Americans believe we're the center of the universe, don't you?" Sam said, returning her smile. "You plan to prove otherwise with the visuals on this globe. Pretty cool idea."

Liza blushed and thanked him.

"Can you top that one, Devlin?" he asked.

"It's not a competition, Sam. I think I chose well, too."

"I'll be the judge of that."

"So my object has to do with Charles Dickens."

"Brava," my mother said to me. She loved great literature and was constantly prodding me to upgrade my reading tastes.

"He had this fascination with taxidermy. Did you know that?"

My mother shook her head.

"He once had a pet raven that he had stuffed after it died and kept in his home. Grip. The raven's name was Grip. He's the very bird that was the inspiration for Edgar Allan Poe's poem."

"Really?" my mother asked, giving me that sideways glance of disbelief.

"Totally true factoid, Mom. There's a lot of correspondence about the raven between Poe and Dickens."

"I don't know where this is going," Sam said, "but probably not in the direction of your mother's bookshelf."

"So Dickens also had a favorite out of all his cats, who sat with him whenever he wrote," I said. "His name was Bob. And when Bob died, Dickens was so heartbroken that he had Bob's paw, well, preserved—you know, stuffed, just like his raven—and made into a letter opener."

My mother poured herself another glass of wine. "The cat's paw?"

"On the blade of the letter opener it's actually engraved 'C.D. In Memory of Bob 1862.' I think that's totally amazing."

"You have such a natural attraction to the bizarre and grotesque," my mother said.

Liza laughed.

"You can't humor her all the time, Liza," my mother joked. "Dev often does things like that just to get attention."

"Not this time, I didn't."

"Where did I go wrong, Dev, darling? There's a Gutenberg Bible in that library's collection. Couldn't you have—?"

"No books, Mom."

"There's Charlotte Brontë's writing desk."

"You know how I feel about the Brontës. Not possible."

"Let it go, Blaine," Sam said. "It's a full-on Devlin Quick. A cat's paw with literary tentacles to Dickens and Poe. You should write your paper in the cadence of 'The Raven,' kid. 'Quoth Charles Dickens, Nevermore.'"

"Totally, Sam. I might do that."

"Okay, now tell your mother exactly why you went to her office afterward."

I whipped my potatoes into a frenzy. "Don't tell me you're a snitch now, Detective Cody. I thought you had my back."

"I'll always have your back, Devlin," Sam said. "I just have to know what's going on in that brain of yours at the same time. When you're on overload, I might need extra guys to keep you covered."

"Today was all my fault, Mr. Cody," Liza said. "It was my idea to report what I saw to the police."

I snapped my head around to look at Liza's face. She was taking the weight so my mother didn't blame me for going overboard. I was impressed. "But, Liza, that's not—"

"Of course it's the truth, Dev," Liza said. "While your daughter was upstairs doing her work, Ms. Quick, I was in the private area of the library called the Map Division."

"I know it well. It's a spectacular room."

"Yes, ma'am. I was examining the famous globe, which was in a glass display case, when I saw this gentleman—"

"He's not a gentleman, Liza," I said. "He's a criminal."

"Well, he had ordered some special book from the librarian, kept behind the counter in the room that the public can't access, and I saw her hand him a pair of cotton gloves and then this oversized book."

"The man walked right past Liza, Mom. Right to the table farthest away from the librarian, in a corner of the room. That's what she told me. Go on, Liza."

When Liza finished reporting her observations, my mother began a rapid-fire series of questions.

"What kind of book was it?"

"I don't know that, Ms. Quick. I couldn't see it."

"What did the knife look like?"

"I—I never saw the actual knife. I just heard the sound of something metal dropping on the floor, right after the man had sliced a page out of the book."

"So you can't say if it was a knife, or a pair of scissors, or a blade of some kind—or a little metal box with breath mints in it—that dropped to the floor?"

"Not exactly."

"You just heard the sound of something metal hitting the floor and you made an assumption," my mother said. "What did the man do with the piece of paper you say he ripped from the book?"

Liza just shrugged and slumped back in her seat.

She was getting the point that she was up against a relentless adversary.

"Did he have a briefcase or a notebook or something to carry this oversized piece of paper in?"

"Look, Mom, we only know what we've told you so far. It's just the beginning of the investigation. We'll figure all that out in time."

"Can you describe the man to me?"

"He was tall," Liza said, "with very pale skin and rimless glasses."

Weird how my memory of the glasses was different from Liza's.

"Anything more than that?"

Liza shook her head.

"Can you do any better than that, Dev?"

"Here's a photograph I took on my phone."

My mother squinted at the image. Then she squinted at me. "Really?"

"That's why we went to your office. I asked Tapp to run it through facial recognition software."

"Use words, Dev. Describe the man to me. You can't rely on an out-of-focus photograph. What kind of features does he have?"

"This is a devastating cross-examination, Commissioner," Sam said, picking up two of the dinner plates and taking them to the sink. "You ought to save that talent for someone your own size, you know what I mean?"

"It's Dev's turn to do the dishes, Sam. If she chooses to play detective, she's got to stand up to the questioning."

"I think you both did exactly the right thing," Sam said to Liza and me. "If more people were as observant as you were today, Liza, there'd be a lot less crime. But you were also smart to tell Sergeant Tapply and the two of us. We'll take over from this point on."

"C'mon, Sam," I said, carrying the rest of the dishes to the sink. "You and Mom are hunting international terrorists and fraudsters and banks that launder money for the bad guys. You'll give this a really low priority. I know you will."

"But I promise you I'll get it assigned, Devlin. Fair enough?"

I hesitated as I filled the sink with soapy water. "Sure, Sam. Sure thing."

"Do you young ladies have homework?" my mother asked.

"Yes, ma'am," Liza said.

"So do I. You're welcome to set up on my table if you want to keep me company."

"An hour of TV when we finish?" I asked.

"Okay. Pick something the three of us can watch together."

Sam was headed for the door. "What time in the morning, Blaine?"

"How is seven forty-five? I'd like to walk the girls over to Ditchley."

"Mom! You're not coming in to complain about Dickens's cat paw, are you?"

"No, dear. I know that would be futile. I just want to spend time with both of you. Make a plan for what we might take Liza to do this weekend."

"Good night, Sam," I said. "See you tomorrow."

I was relieved that my mother wasn't going to get in the way of our case investigation. If I zipped through tonight's homework fast enough, I'd be able to do an Internet search about book thieves. I needed some focus for our investigation. It had never occurred to me before today that danger could be lurking in the public library.

5

"Thanks for trying to take the blame for what I did today, Liza," I said as I got into bed and pulled the sheet up to cover me. We had done our homework, walked the dog together, and watched the rerun of an old TV show.

"No reason for you to get in trouble for what I started," she said. "Did you finish all the readings about the French Revolution?"

"Yes." I reached out and turned off the lamp that was on the narrow nightstand between our beds. "And I had time to check something out online, too. Get this. There's an organization called the Latitude Society."

"What is it?"

"All the members are interested in maps and cartography and rare books that have drawings of antique maps in them. That's where I'll start my research, I think."

"Can anyone use the society to get information?"

"Oh, no. You have to be a member. It's normally very expensive, but students get a really big discount."

"So you joined?"

"Nope. I signed *you* up for membership, Liza. You're the one who knows about globes and all that stuff. I promise I'll pay for it out of my allowance."

She was quiet.

"Do you mind if I ask you some questions, Dev? I mean, personal ones."

"No problem." I figured I owed her that much. And I had spent a lot of last night asking her about her family, so I expected curiosity in return.

I had learned that both her parents were schoolteachers, which helped account for her being such a brainiac. She was a scholarship student at the American School in Buenos Aires, just as she was for this summer program at the Ditch. Liza had two older sisters and a younger brother, the kind of sibling connections that always sounded so good to an only child.

"Is that man Sam your mother's boyfriend?" she asked.

"In my dreams."

"Then what?"

"Every police commissioner, just like a lot of officials in government, has a 'detail.' That's what it's called in the department. Mom has to be body-guarded twenty-four/seven. Like right now, there's a patrol car parked in front of our building for over-night, so that there is always protection for my mother."

"Sam is part of that detail?"

"My mother used to be a federal prosecutor, Liza. She handled some of the major cases that were based in this city—things that I wasn't supposed to know about when I was just a kid, but now I've read most of the clippings and understand how serious they were."

I was probably four or five when my mother met Sam Cody. Like her, he was tall and lean, and like her, he had straight blond hair. Sometimes I thought they resembled a brother and sister, which is mostly how they acted.

"Sam is a first-grade detective. He works homicide. There was this terrible case seven years ago that was a joint investigation with the feds and local prosecutors."

"What kind of case?"

"A bunch of really bad guys were kidnapping teenagers in the poorest parts of Europe and bringing them to America with promises of a better life."

"Better how?"

"That they would have jobs in upstate New York, mostly farming and working in fields. Once these teens got here, in some horrible freight ship, they were held by these guys and actually kept like slaves."

"You mean trafficking?"

"Yes, that's exactly what I mean," I said. "Sam was in charge of the NYPD part of the task force, because several of the young men died trying to escape from the freighter to a beach in Queens when they could see how they were being treated. My mother ran the prosecution, and she and Sam became best friends. Have been ever since."

"How old is your mother?" Liza asked.

"Forty-four. The first woman to be police commissioner in New York, and not all the men on the force like that idea. It's not one of the great feminist strongholds in the country. But Mayor Bloomfield thinks the world of her, and he took the chance to make her PC."

"Awesome."

"Sam is two years younger than she is. He's divorced now, with two sons—eight-year-old twins. My mother trusts him with her life, so she asked him to run her detail."

"They won their case?"

"Yeah, the bad guys are away forever, I think." I rolled onto my side to face Liza. "That's also how Natasha came into our lives."

"How?"

"She was one of those girls, Liza. From Moldova, in the former Soviet Union. She was orphaned in her country when she was our age, so when her friends introduced her to the men making promises about how much better things would be in America, she thought she had nothing to lose by coming here."

"Natasha was a witness in your mother's case?"

"She was. And when it was over, she was supposed to go to a foster home. But after everything she'd been through, and all the abuse she'd experienced, she just couldn't start over with strangers. She and my mother had grown close during the case and they both thought that maybe Natasha could try coming to live with us. So my mother asked her boss if it was possible. And after they worked it out, Natasha got into a good school, and Mom hired a tutor to help her learn English. She's lived with us ever since, and she's become part of our family. She was always there to watch over me when I was little, so I love her like a sister. Even though it means that now I have two adults I have to listen to!"

"That's amazing. Such a generous thing for your mother to do."

"It's Natasha who's amazing. She's kind of like my best friend in the world, even though she's twenty-two years old. She finished high school and now she's got one more year at Columbia till she graduates with a degree in history."

"You know what I like best about all this?" Liza said to me. "It's the way your mother has created a family for both of you. You said you were so envious of me having sisters and a brother, but you've got Sam and Natasha and Tapp, and I'm sure there are others. You've got a real family, Dev."

I looked away, toward the wall, fighting back tears that seemed to well up out of nowhere. I'd give anything just to have my father be alive, even though

I loved all the surrogates my mother had gathered around us.

"Dev," Liza spoke softly into the darkness of the small room, "how did your father die?"

I cleared my throat to answer. "He was a journalist. At least that's what his credentials said. Working for the *Wall Street Journal* when he met my mom. But my grandmother thinks he was a spy, working for the CIA. She says that investigative journalism was just a front for him to get access to people."

"A spy? Really?"

"That's one of the things she argues about with my mother, who tells her not to fill my head with those absurd stories."

"They met through her work?"

"Yes, they did. It's a really sweet love story," I said, even though there were days I couldn't bear to hear it, knowing how his death had broken my mother's heart and spirit. "They got married five months before my father died in an explosion in Paris. My mother was pregnant with me. No one has ever been caught."

Liza was quiet. I was hoping she had run out of questions.

"Is that why you're taking a journalism course

in the fall?" she asked after a couple of minutes of silence. "To do your father's kind of work?"

"No way. I want to be exactly like my mother when I get older. Go to college at Vassar, then law school, then get a job as a prosecutor in the Manhattan District Attorney's Office, working my way up to the feds."

"Oh, Dev. That must make her so proud, so happy to know."

I reached for the tissue box on the night table and blew my nose. "Are you kidding? I'd never tell her that at this point. It would go directly to her head, Liza. She'd be insufferable with me."

Liza laughed. "That could never happen."

"This way I can learn by stealth. I know how she thinks and study what she says and pick up all kinds of techniques every day that I'm around her. Better that she believes I want to be a forensic biologist for now, which isn't a bad second choice."

I wanted to become the best investigator I could possibly be, and no one was a better example to follow than my mother. And when I grew up, I was determined to track down the people who killed my father.

6

My alarm went off at seven a.m. Liza and I dressed for school and went into the kitchen. My mother was on her third cup of coffee, by the looks of the water level in the coffeemaker. She had a stack of newspapers next to her, and I leaned over to give her a kiss. It was her habit to walk Asta early in the morning, and the sweet dog was sitting at her feet, hoping for crumbs.

"Good morning. How did you girls sleep?"

"Very well, Ms. Quick," Liza said.

"English muffin, Liza?" I asked. I poured us each a glass of orange juice and put the muffins in the toaster. "Mom?"

"I've been up since five. Two days away from my desk and I had a lot to catch up on. I've eaten, thanks."

"Do you ever wear a uniform, Ms. Quick?"

I think Liza was taking in my mother's navy blue pin-striped suit with its pencil skirt, and the spiky high heels that stuck out from under the end of the table. She looked more like she was on her way to work at a fashion magazine than police headquarters.

"No, dear. I get to wear my civilian clothes. One of my job perks."

"Sam's her biggest perk," I said, grinning at my mother as I pushed the toaster controls down to make the muffins crisper. "Isn't he?"

"Yours and mine both, Dev. Could we have a better friend? His ex-wife took the twins upstate for the summer, to her parents' home. He's really feeling down, so I want to include him in things that we do. Try not to bug him, will you?"

"Promise."

"Would you like to know what happened in the world while you were sleeping?"

Mom liked to start each morning this way. She thought there was nothing that would ever replace black-and-white newsprint. She devoured the big stories and all the little news bits in every paper left on our doorstep. I scanned the Internet instead— so much faster and up to the minute—because we always got quizzed on current events at the Ditch.

"Give us the good news first, Mom."

"There actually isn't anything terrible on the front pages. There's a story about Argentina and the next election that might interest you, Liza, and a nice piece about the summer Olympics."

"No earthquakes? No tsunamis? No tornadoes?" I asked. Catastrophic events and extreme weather freaked me out. I couldn't wrap my brain about why those things always happened somewhere else and not here. I spent way too much time worrying about when our day would come.

"None."

But what my mother was really looking for were crime stories—what had happened in the last twenty-four hours that she might have to address. Heads would roll if commanding officers in Brooklyn or Queens had not called in any patterns of serial criminals or especially vulnerable victims. When she got to the office, her first call of the day would be to the mayor of the city, and she had to know more than he did about the safety of his streets.

"Any homicides last night?" I asked.

"No, Sherlock. We've really brought the murder rate way down, as you know," Mom said, then turned to Liza. "Years ago, violent crime was a huge issue in this city. There was a day when people like your parents would never have sent their child here for a month."

"Yes, ma'am. My father was actually at university here in the late 1980s, when it was a rougher city. He's told us lots of stories."

"I hope you'll be able to impress him with how far we've come by the time we've shown you around New York this month," my mother said, pushing back from the table. "Out the door in five, okay?"

I carried the dishes to the sink and rinsed them. "Where's Natasha?"

Natasha was very wise, and I thought I could consult her about the theft. But I loved that she had a group of good friends at school and could hang out with them in her free time. She had been so shy when she first came to live with us.

"Sleeping in. She got home late. Grab your books and let's go."

The three of us rode down in the elevator and through the lobby. The building on East Eighty-Third Street was a bit shabby looking, nothing a good coat of paint in the public areas couldn't improve. The PD didn't make a fuss about the building's security, since there was a doorman on duty twenty-four hours a day, supported by the uniformed detail outside.

Sam was leaning against the black SUV that was my mother's "on the job" car.

It was a beautiful June morning, and he was sipping a cup of coffee, having relieved the midnight detail by his arrival.

"Can I ride with Sam, Mom?"

"We're walking, sweetheart. I'll be cooped up in my office all day."

I looped my arm in hers after she handed Sam two tote bags full of papers and police reports. She hooked her other arm with Liza, and the three of us headed off toward East End Avenue, where the Ditchley School had established itself ninety years ago on some of Manhattan's prime real estate overlooking the East River.

"What do you two say to Shakespeare in the Park on Saturday evening?" my mother asked.

"What a cool idea!" Liza said. "Central Park? I'd love to go there. It's supposed to be so beautiful."

"I was thinking of maybe a Yankees game, Mom. Show Liza the all-American sport. Hot dogs and peanuts and the stadium."

"I think they're playing in town next weekend. I'll check."

One thing about being police commissioner, my mother sometimes got outrageously good tickets for sporting events, probably because the parks commissioner lost one of the friendly bets they were always wagering. We were at the stadium on opening day in April, sitting directly behind the dugout, and I scored autographs from half the team.

"Don't you like Shakespeare, Dev?" Liza asked.

She kept looking over her shoulder, watching Sam crawl along in the SUV about ten feet behind us. I was so used to having a shadow at our backs everywhere we went that I hadn't noticed him at all.

"We haven't had much of him yet in class. The one I like best so far is *Macbeth*."

"Of course you would," my mother said. "A dark tragedy featuring a trio of witches. Throw in some murder and madness. Dev is obsessed with murder, in case you haven't noticed."

I wasn't going to stick anything in my mother's face, but I had good reason to be obsessed with murder. She'd dealt with my dad's death by devoting herself to advocacy for victims of all types of crimes. She'd worked out some of her anguish that way, I'm sure. It was all much more raw for me, the great big hole in my life driving so much of my emotional reaction to things.

"*Romeo and Juliet*. That's Saturday's play."

"It's my favorite, Ms. Quick," Liza said. "I've read it twice and seen the ballet."

"Sappy," I murmured. "Star-crossed lovers and all that. Dripping with sap."

My mother pinched my forearm. "Would you still think so if I tell you that Bradley Cooper is playing Romeo and Jennifer Lawrence is Juliet?"

"What?" I said, breaking free to run ahead so I could turn to face my mother.

"And if you're not too upset about my choice of a play, I can ask the producer if it might be possible to go backstage and meet the cast after the performance."

"That is the coolest thing ever, Mom," I said, jumping toward her and throwing my arms around her neck.

"You are so fickle, Devlin Quick," she said. "I'm only asking about getting backstage because Liza is here. Otherwise I wouldn't want to spoil you constantly. And also, I'll allow it if you stop nosing into business where you don't belong."

"Well, the swordplay is really fun to watch and the balcony scene is a hoot," I said, changing the subject.

"I think you'll like the entire plan, Liza," my mother said. "We'll go as a small group with some of our friends—we do it every year—and we'll picnic on the grass in the park before the show. In fact, we can take you on a tour of Central Park beforehand, so you can see the zoo and Literary Walk and Bethesda Terrace. The show is done in an open-air theater, and it's quite a wonderful summer tradition in New York."

"Thank you so much, Ms. Quick. It sounds really exciting."

I ran to the SUV and grabbed onto Sam's arm, which was on the window frame. "Will you come to Shakespeare with us on Saturday night?"

"Are you my date, Devlin?"

"If Bradley Cooper won't have me."

"Yes. Your mother invited me already."

I ran back to her side. "Who else?"

"Natasha's coming, too, with one of her friends. And Booker, if he stays in town."

"Booker!" I exclaimed. Why hadn't I thought to involve Booker Dibble in our investigation?

"Who is he?" Liza asked.

"Only my best friend in the world."

"I thought that was Katie?"

"Booker's my best *guy* friend. His mother was my mother's college roommate, so I've known him since I was born. We've spent every Thanksgiving and Christmas together, and a lot of our vacations."

"See, Dev? Another sibling for you," Liza said. "You have to stop whining about being an only."

"He certainly is like that. But he has two older brothers—real ones—and now that he's almost thirteen he'd rather spend time with them. And with girls he doesn't have to treat like they're his sisters."

"You'll meet him Saturday night," my mother said.

Maybe before that, I thought. Katie Cion had texted me late last night that her parents wouldn't let her come back into the city from Montauk simply because I thought I was on the trail of a thief. Booker was a different story. He liked capers as much as I did.

"This is as far as I go, sweetheart," my mother said when we reached the corner of East End Avenue. She gave us each a kiss and reminded me to forget about my extracurricular activities and ace the summer courses.

By the time Liza and I reached the front steps of the school, the SUV was out of sight. We walked inside, did the obligatory curtsy in front of the enormous portrait of the late Wilhelmina Ditchley, and said the words of her motto, WE LEARN, WE LEAD, which had been implanted in the brains of her girls for more generations than I could count.

Liza and I had three classes to get through before we continued our research—and snooping—at the NYPL. We were both in the World Culture class which had spawned the assignment at the library, and together again in the second hour for European history, which was all about the French Revolution this week.

We split up for the third class, which was my favorite. The school librarian, Doris Shorey, had been at the Ditch for almost fifty years. She'd been my one steady teacher since first grade and had instilled in me a love for reading, for everything about books.

Some of my earliest memories are of my mother sitting beside me in bed, reading to me from colorful board books and then the singsong poetry of Robert Louis Stevenson. Every night, before I had to face the dark and try to sleep, I had three stories read to me. But then she got a much more high-powered position at work, and there were a string of nannies before Natasha came along. Not all of them were enthusiastic about reading, and Natasha's English made it a struggle for the first two years she was with us.

Miss Shorey opened my mind to the wonders of storytelling. The Ditchley library looked like a room in an English castle, out of Hogwarts, with fine wood trim and huge windows that were flooded with light most of the day. In the corner closest to the river was a wing chair covered in dark green leather. Every Friday, one of the girls was chosen to spend the class hour reading in that chair. It's in that small oasis—the green chair in the sunny corner of the room—that I met Huck Finn and Pippi Longstocking, the Artful Dodger and Hercule Poirot. That great librarian put each of those books in my hungry hands.

And on those days when the school got a call that the police commissioner was working late and Natasha was stuck in class, I was allowed to go to Miss Shorey's room, to her cozy green chair, and make friends with all the wonderful characters who live in books, while I waited for someone to greet me at home.

Miss Shorey taught a summer school class in literature, and she was as happy to have me enrolled as I was to be there. Only eight students took the course, which gave us all a lot of one-on-one time with Miss

Shorey. This week's assignment was an introduction to Jane Austen in *Pride and Prejudice*, which was a lot more fun than I thought it was going to be based on my experience with those other British girls.

The first two classes dragged for me, but I hated for this hour to end.

"Thank you, Miss Shorey," I said as I packed up to leave. "I'm really liking *Pride and Prejudice*."

"I thought you'd enjoy it, Dev," the petite woman with short snow-white hair said to me. "Such a smart writer, and so witty. There's going to be an exhibit of Austen's personal correspondence in town this fall. I think I'll make it a class trip so you can all see the letters in her own handwriting."

"At the New York Public Library? We're doing a project there for our World Culture class right now. It's where I'm going after lunch. I'm writing a paper about Charles Dickens's stuffed cat's paw."

"Ah, poor Bob!"

"Then you know about it?"

"I could live in that library if they'd allow it, Dev. So many treasures there. If you want to get ahead of the class," Miss Shorey said with a smile, "the assignment for our last week is going to be the novel *Frankenstein*."

"You totally rock!"

"Devlin Quick. You know better—"

"I'm sorry, Miss Shorey." In her delightfully old-fashioned way, she had banned the word 'awesome' and its related offspring from her classes. "That's a great idea. You're making the summer so much fun for us, as well as interesting."

"Imagine, Dev, that a novel written two hundred years ago, by a woman, is still borrowed in every art form from literature to film to stage plays," Miss Shorey said.

"That's so cool. She didn't have to do it in summer school, did she?" I said with a laugh.

"Better than that, there was a contest between Percy Shelley and Lord Byron—two of our greatest poets—and Mary Shelley, who later married Percy Shelley, was in the contest with them."

"What kind of contest?"

"To see which one could write the best horror story."

"And it was Mary who won?"

"That's right. A bit of my purpose is to make the summer session enjoyable, but also to light some fires in your literary brains," Miss Shorey said. "Jane Austen was twenty when she wrote her first novel,

Dev. Mary Shelley was only eighteen years old when she created the Frankenstein monster. Heavens, you'll all be eighteen by the time you leave Ditchley, and I intend to have some completed manuscripts from a few of you by graduation."

I laughed. "I'd better get busy."

"When the curators let you see Bob's paw this afternoon, ask them for a look at a lock of Mary Shelley's hair. That's also in the library collection. Better still, Dev. Take a picture of her hair, too. Print it out and hold it in your locker here until we get to discuss her. Then you'll have something to show the others."

"Thanks for the tip, Miss Shorey. See you tomorrow."

I was completely energized by her idea. Not the part about Mary Shelley's long-dead hair, which seemed as bizarre to keep around as a cat's stuffed paw, but the tip that reminded me that my locker—which was assigned to me for the entire school year—had something in it from last semester that could prove useful to Liza and me in working our case.

7

Liza was waiting for me by Miss Ditchley's portrait.

"Sorry to be late, but my teacher just reminded me of something I've got in my locker. You can wait for me here or—"

"I'm coming with you, Dev."

I took the stairs two at a time, another unladylike action that Miss Ditchley would have frowned upon. My locker was two-thirds of the way down the hall, and I raced ahead of Liza to get to it. I punched in the four numbers that opened the digital lock.

There was a set of dirty gym clothes that I had forgotten to take home when classes ended, but they would last another day without being washed. I had notebooks for each subject—English, math, French, biology, and American history—and then there were folders stacked on the top shelf with a miscellaneous assortment of stuff.

"What are you looking for?" Liza asked. "I can go through part of the pile if you tell me what you need."

I grabbed a couple of inches of folders and gave the other half of them to Liza. "We had this project in the spring to bring to our history class two pieces of paper that were, well, I think 'unique' was the word the teacher used. Something no one else might have at home. Each of them," I said, sitting down on the floor to spread out the files, "was supposed to lead us to discuss some aspect of history related to the paper."

"So what's my search?" Liza asked, sitting beside me.

"I brought a piece of carbon paper, and—"

"Carbon paper? What's that?"

"My mother's suggestion, really. She told me what it was, and I thought it would be an interesting look at how the invention of computers have changed the world. It didn't spark quite the conversation as Katie's special paper—a handwritten letter to her grandfather from President Kennedy, which was the best thing in the whole class—but none of the kids had ever seen carbon paper."

I was flipping through the folders too quickly, so I slowed myself down. "A long time ago, Liza, before there were computers and printers, everything was either written by hand or on a typewriter."

"Sure."

"In order to make duplicates of the pages, there was this thing called carbon paper. The top side was shiny and usually had printing on it with the name of the company who made it. The one I brought was sort of a red-and-silver metallic design. The bottom side was coated with dry ink—a purplish blue—so you could make copies by putting it between the page you were writing or typing on, and a blank paper beneath it."

"I've never seen a piece of it," Liza said, sifting through the assorted papers.

"I hadn't, either. There isn't even a sheet, I don't think, in the entire Puzzle Palace. But my mother used to know this great secretary at the city prosecutor's office—she's got to be in her seventies—and Mom remembered that she still kept a box in her desk drawer, just for nostalgia."

"So red-and-silver metallic and kind of purplish blue. I'm looking. Okay, what's the second one?"

"The day I went downtown to pick up the carbon

paper at the courthouse, I had another idea for an unusual piece of paper," I said. "A grand jury subpoena."

"What's that, exactly?"

"It's a small piece of paper, in this case you're looking for something about eight inches long by four inches high, and it's green."

Liza was nodding as she reapplied herself to looking for the subpoena.

She didn't seem to get the direction I was heading in, which was probably a good thing.

"That must have been interesting for the other kids. Did anyone else have a parent who used to be a prosecutor?"

"Nope. It was the first time all of them had ever seen one."

"Here's the carbon paper," Liza said.

"Watch out. That ink on the bottom side will get all over your hands," I said. "Now find the subpoena and we're good to go."

"What is it that a subpoena does?"

"It's a court summons, ordering a person to appear at a trial. Once you get served a subpoena by a district attorney or a police officer, you have to show up or the judge can punish you."

"Don't tell me you think you're actually going to serve it on the thief if we run into him?"

"Not a bad idea at all, Liza, but that's not my plan."

"I've got it!" Liza said, practically shouting at me, waving the paper in my face. "It says *Subpoena Duces Tecum*."

"How's your Latin?"

"Pretty good, actually. I had to learn it for church. It's a subpoena for the production of evidence."

"That should work perfectly."

"Work for what?" Liza asked.

"Like I said, there is another kind of subpoena that directs a person to appear and testify at trial. We don't need that type, Liza."

"Because . . . ?" She had that puzzled frown dragging down her entire face.

"I just want to show this one so the Map Division librarian gives us the actual book—that would be the production of real evidence—that the thief tore the page from. You know what a call slip is?"

"Of course I do," Liza said, almost in a whisper.

I didn't want her going all limp on me, losing her backbone just when we needed to stand tall together.

"In order to get a book in that library, you have to fill out a call slip, with the title of the volume and the author's name on it. I wish the books were just lying around on shelves like they are at an ordinary library."

"But we don't even know the name of the book," Liza said, standing up.

"Yes, but we do know the date and the exact time the man got the book yesterday afternoon. This is a piece of cake," I said. "With that subpoena, I just get to pretend that I'm part of the summer education program they run at the DA's office."

"What will you do with the book?"

"The lab that does all the city's DNA work for the police department is at the Office of the Chief Medical Examiner. I've been there dozens of times with my mother. The head of the lab actually came to Ditchley with me to show the biology class how DNA is extracted from evidence and used to solve crimes. I've got lots of buddies at the lab."

Liza couldn't even look me in the eye.

"All we have to do is put the book in a large brown supermarket shopping bag—never put evidence in plastic—and we take it to the lab. We'll get it jumped to the front of the line for examination. C'mon."

Liza didn't budge.

"What's the problem?" I asked.

"First of all, we promised your mother and Sam that we wouldn't do anything more about the book thief, okay? That's the most important thing."

"I agree with you. There's nothing more important than my relationship with my mother. But I don't think you get how much she really values independence, that she likes me to make decisions for myself and then act on them."

"Well, it's pretty clear she wants us to drop our investigation."

I shook my head. "I think she only meant I shouldn't do anything dangerous, you know, like chasing the man into the train station."

"Dev, that's not a fiblet. That's just a bald-faced lie," Liza said. "And so is handing a subpoena to a total stranger and pretending to work for the district attorney. What do you plan to do, write the prosecutor's signature on the document on top of all that?"

"Not necessary," I said. "That would be forgery. If you look at the bottom right side of the green paper, you'll see it already has his signature stamp on it. District Attorney Cyrus Chance. I'd never monkey with that."

"But you're not in a summer program in his office."

"I could have been, Liza. The kids get to sit in court

and watch trials, which I was really keen to do, but then my mother insisted on summer school. We get speedy action from the DNA lab and the scientists forward the results to DA Chance. He and my mother's crew will make the case."

I held my hand out for the paper, but Liza wouldn't give it to me.

"Third," she said, "is to remind you that if the book is so valuable that someone is stealing pages from it, you think we're going to walk out of the secure library and get on the subway with it, without an armed guard? It's probably worth thousands of dollars."

Liza was three for three in her arguments. Nobody ever said she was stupid.

"Now what are you doing, Dev?" Liza said in a voice that barely hid her frustration with me.

"I'm texting Booker Dibble," I said, punching in the letters to say where RU? "To meet us at the library after we have lunch, if he's around."

"But why?" Liza said in a voice a little too close to a whine for my taste.

"A fresh set of eyes on the situation, Liza. That's always a good thing."

The text balloon opened with Booker's reply. Just finished tennis camp. U?

Meet me and my friend at the NYPL at 2:30? Need help with a case.

C U. there. So the game is afoot, huh?

I laughed as I texted him yes.

"What's so funny?" Liza asked as we retraced our steps to the door of Ditchley.

"Booker and I love the Arthur Conan Doyle stories. We both like to solve things the way Sherlock Holmes would. He texted me back that the game is afoot. I'm just laughing cause that's so Sherlockian."

I watched out of a corner of my eye as Liza folded up the subpoena and put it in her pocket.

"That's a Shakespearean phrase, actually. From *Henry IV*," Liza said. "Long before Conan Doyle used it."

"You may be right about the subpoena, Liza," I said. "But you don't have to be right about everything."

8

Liza and I stopped for a sandwich on Eighty-Sixth Street before getting on the subway to go downtown to the library.

"So is Booker Dibble your boyfriend?" Liza asked as we walked from Grand Central to the feet of the library lions.

"What is it about you getting up into everyone's business about boyfriends? First my mother, now me. I'm way too young to have a boyfriend," I said. "Why, do you?"

"No, but I think about it a lot. Too much, maybe, my mother says."

"Even when I think about it, it's kind of hopeless. Like the way I said nobody wants to do sleepovers because Tapp runs a background check on them? Imagine a guy invites me to go to a movie with him, while some uniformed cop comes along for the date. Besides, every guy our age, except Booker, is at least a head shorter than I am. We have dances every year with the all-boys' schools. I might as well bring along a giraffe if I want to do a slow dance."

"So, what should I know about Booker?"

"Like I said, he's my best guy friend. He'll be thirteen in December, so even though he's only six months older than me he thinks he's way cooler."

"Which boys' school does he go to?"

"He doesn't. Booker and his brothers have all gone to Hunter, a magnet school."

"Is his mother a lawyer, too?"

"Nope. Both his parents are doctors. His father's a neurosurgeon and his mother's an orthopedic surgeon. My mother jokes that the reason she likes us going on ski vacations with the Dibbles is that they'd be in charge of all my survival needs," I said. "I'm a really lousy skier."

"I've never skied," Liza said. "What's your sport?"

"Swimming's my favorite. The Ditch has a great pool, and a mediocre swim team. But I'm on it. You?"

"Soccer's my best. I'm a pretty fast sprinter, too. I tried out—"

"There's Booker!"

"Where?"

"The tall African American kid at the top of the steps in the baseball cap and jeans."

"Now I see him."

Maybe Liza was a sprinter, but she seemed glued to her spot once she took a look at Booker. So I dashed up the steps to greet him.

"Hey! I'm so glad you could shake free to meet me here."

"Hey, Dev! What's up?" Booker said, wrapping one of his long arms around my back, pulling me into a hug.

"Same old, same old." I turned to reach out a hand to Liza. "I want you to meet my new friend, Liza de Lucena. Liza, this is Booker."

Her eyes lit up and Liza pumped his hand, clearly happy to meet an almost-teenaged boy.

"What's the problem?" Booker asked.

"Come inside to the lobby and we'll explain."

It only took a few minutes to brief Booker on the situation. Just as I expected, he was completely ready to be part of our team.

"Show Booker the subpoena, Liza."

She withdrew it from her pocket—reluctantly, it seemed to me—and handed it to him. Booker studied the legal language, then held the subpoena in front of my face and ripped it in half.

"Booker!"

"Not happening, Dev. Liza's right."

"She's only afraid that we'll get caught doing something wrong. You can't live just being driven by fear."

"I'm not afraid, Dev. I'm just telling you to do the right thing," Booker said. "Is your moral compass out of whack for the moment? You can't serve a real subpoena when you're a twelve-year-old kid with no legal authority."

"I thought it was a bold idea," I said, smiling at both of them. "Creative."

"Haven't you got a backup plan?"

"Calling you was my backup plan, Booker. We always seem to figure something out," I said, scratching my head. "Wait, something's growing on me."

"Shoot."

"How about we try a straight approach to the librarian who runs the Map Division? Liza and I will go into the room with you. There's this famous globe that she's writing her school paper about. It's in a glass case, and we can create a diversion by making a big deal about it."

"Cool project," Booker said, flashing a grin at Liza.

I thought that the glue holding her braces in place might melt. Booker is like a brother to me, but there's no question he's totally hot to most other girls.

"You go to the librarians' desk. Liza thinks there's a large ledger where you sign in if you're going to request books. If that's on the counter, you can check the names from yesterday and write them on a pad, and sign yourself in, too, to be safe."

"Easy enough. What book am I going to request?" Booker Dibble always wanted a real plan.

I looked at Liza. "You know the names of any important map books? We'll need a cover for Booker to be working with."

She reached for her cell phone and clicked on its search engine. "I'll pull up a few titles in the library's collection."

"What else?" Booker asked.

"It depends on how many names are on yesterday's list. If there are just three or four people who were in there doing research, maybe Liza and I can figure out which one might be our tall man by the time of day he was here. If there's a long list, we have to narrow it down to identify the right man—and the book he defaced. The lady will probably give you a pair of cotton gloves before she lets you handle any books."

"Gloves?"

"Everything in the map collection is rare and valuable. They're written and drawn on vellum or really old paper that's very delicate. Act like you're used to using gloves, like you're a scholar."

"Got it, Dev."

"Okay. Now let's go into the gift shop for a minute," I said. The NYPL had the neatest gift shop in the lobby, selling all kinds of things with book designs on them or related to reading. "We need a few props."

"Like what?" Booker asked.

"You need a notebook and—"

"A pen."

"Pencils only in the Map Division," Liza said.

"She's right. These research libraries make you do all your note taking in pencil, so there is no chance of getting ink stains on the paper."

"Okay, so what else?"

"They sell reading glasses. Eighteen dollars."

"You know I don't need glasses, Dev," Booker said.

"Right now you look like a total jock," I said. "You need to put spectacles on the tip of your nose, so you look more like an earnest student."

"How much money do you have?" Booker asked me.

"Twenty-two dollars."

"I've got fifteen," Liza said.

"I've got eighteen," Booker said. "We're good for glasses, I guess."

When we came out of the shop, I ripped the tags off the glasses—serious-looking black frames—and armed Booker with his pad and pencil.

"Give us three minutes," I said. "The Map Division is at the far corner of the hallway here, on the right. It's not very big at all. The librarians stand behind a counter to your right. There are only ever one or two of them, and we'll be very close by, across the room."

"Globe-trotting," he said with a nod to Liza.

"Right."

"Is there a reason that I'm doing this and not you?" Booker asked as he adjusted the glasses on his nose.

"Of course there is."

"Because I'm smarter than you are, Devlin Quick. Right?"

"How dare you say that to a Ditchley girl?" I asked with mock outrage. "It's because you're charming. I'm capable of being charming, Booker, but I can't always pull it off at will. And in addition to that rare combination of intelligence and charm, you've got several inches of height on me. That will allow the librarian to take you seriously and believe you're familiar with—give us some titles, Liza?"

"Gerard Mercator's *Atlas of the New World*. Two volumes. Ninety-five maps, including every country known in the seventeenth century except for Transylvania. You could ask for that one," she said. "It's one of the library's great treasures. Or anything by Johann Bayer. Like his *Atlas of the Celestial Spheres*."

Liza reeled off four other names, and Booker took a moment to enter the list into his cell phone.

"Can you be familiar with those?" I asked Booker. "And hand me your baseball cap. I'll keep it in my tote."

"I can't believe how bossy you are," Liza said as Booker handed over the cap.

"Bossy? Haven't you met Dev's mother yet? There's nothing about Dev that I can't handle, but my aunt Blaine? We're not even really related, but she still orders me around more than my mom."

That description sort of surprised Liza. I could tell by the expression on her face.

"By the way, Dev," Booker asked with a smile, "do I know you?"

"Never saw you before in my life," I said, turning my back to him. "We're going in."

I stuffed the cap in my tote, and Liza and I marched down the long hallway to the Map Division. I pulled back on one of the two heavy doors, and she followed me inside.

I looked to my right and saw one librarian behind the desk. There were six or seven people spread out at the long tables in the center of the room, each of them studying maps or books. I paused while Liza passed by to lead me to the empty end of one table that was closest to the glass-encased globe that she had chosen to study.

A couple of minutes later, Booker walked into the room. He glanced around and then went directly to the desk. I couldn't believe how grown up he looked with his new glasses on and the collar of his polo shirt turned up.

The room was dead quiet, as a library should be. But I couldn't hear him speak to the woman at the desk, so I stood up and got closer, examining a large wall map of 1878 Manhattan.

"Do you have your student identification?" the woman asked Booker. She was about my height, with frizzy brown hair and glasses that hung from a chain around her neck.

"Sure," he said, removing it from his wallet and handing it to her.

"Hunter College High School," she said, looking up from the photograph to stare at Booker's face, smiling broadly as she did. "Well, that tells me you must be bright, which is a good beginning for our relationship, Mr. Dibble. Bright students and curious ones are my favorite patrons."

Even though he was only about to enter eighth grade, the school run by Hunter College and the city's Department of Education started in seventh grade, but was called a high school.

Way to go, I thought. It hadn't occurred to me that just the name of the institution would add years to Booker's presentation.

"It's a tough program," he said to her, "and a good one."

"Getting ready for college, are you?"

"Yes, ma'am."

Only five grades to go, Booker.

"Do you have a library pass, too?"

"Sure. I've never been in the Map Division before,

but my teachers all send us to the NYPL for assignments. This time I got lucky. I know you have a great collection."

"We certainly do. I'm Martha Bland, Mr. Dibble. How can I help you today?"

"I'd like to begin with an atlas, Ms. Bland. I'd like to have a look at Gerard Mercator's *Geographic Description of the World*. I think it's the 1636 edition I want. Two volumes, ninety-five maps?"

"Well, that's starting at the top, young man," she said. "I guess that you've got a serious interest in maps if you want to see that particular atlas."

"A recent interest," Booker said. "Recent but serious."

Truer words were never spoken.

"Mercator is always popular here, Mr. Dibble. He coined the word 'atlas,' if you didn't know that. But there must be something special going on."

"Really?"

"These volumes are usually kept off-site. They're the kind of rarities that you need to call for and order in advance, which is just a piece of advice I have for you going forward."

"That will be helpful. Thanks so much for telling me."

"But I've had three people in this week—two of them yesterday—who wanted the very same volumes," Ms. Bland said. "It's probably the most valuable atlas in the world."

9

"Here's a pair of gloves for you, Mr. Dibble," the librarian said, reaching under the counter and coming up with the white cotton page protectors. "Settle yourself down at a table, and I'll go back and search for the Mercator."

"Wouldn't you like me to sign in, Ms. Bland?" Booker asked. "I was instructed to sign your log. I know you must keep very accurate records."

"We'll get to that. Not to worry."

She walked away to the secured area where all the books were stored. I went back to my seat and made room for Booker in the middle of the long table, closest to Liza.

"Dude, you are the man," I whispered to him. "College-bound map scholar, as of the last hour, and Ms. Bland is buying into your entire act."

Booker opened his notebook and started to write

in it. "What happens when she brings me a Mercator atlas?" he asked. "Then what do I do?"

"I never thought you'd get it this fast," I said. "I thought she'd hassle you and we'd have time with the sign-in book. We have to get the tall man's name right before we can figure out what book he was ruining."

"If she brings the book instead of the sign-in log, what am I looking for?"

"A missing page."

"Well, how do I find it if it's missing, Dev? If it's not there, I won't know it's not there, right? Use your brain."

"I saw the man slice a page from a book," Liza said. "I don't know which book, but there should be a sliver of paper left that attached the page into the binding of the book."

"Why would someone do something like that?" Booker asked.

"Could be he's just a crazy person," Liza said, "or could be there's something valuable on that particular page."

"How valuable could a single page be?" he said.

"Here she comes," I said to Liza. "Let's get up and look at your globe."

Martha Bland was carrying a very oversized book. She had cotton gloves on, too, and was holding it in her arms, which were stretched out in front of her with the big book on its side, like she was making an offering of something precious to Booker.

She rested the book on the table, right next to the seat where I had placed my tote bag.

"Here you go, Mr. Dibble," she said. "Mercator's *Atlas of the World*. Volume One."

"Thanks so much, ma'am," he said as she swiveled it around to face him.

"Now, exactly what is it you're looking for?" I heard her say as I leaned in toward the globe and pretended to whisper something to Liza about it.

"My—uh, my instructions were sort of just to spend the first afternoon exploring the book," he said. "Turning the pages and enjoying the history of it."

"That's a wise approach," the librarian said. "But I've got good news and there's bad news for you. Which would you like to hear first?"

"I'll take the good news," Booker said with a smile.

"That's the spirit," she said, sitting down opposite him, keeping one eye on her desk, in case of another visitor. "This is one of the most extraordinary books in the world."

Martha Bland reached across and opened the cover of the atlas. She turned pages until she reached the first map, and Booker let out a whistle as he lowered his head to look at it.

"Is that the book you saw yesterday?" I asked Liza.

"I can't be sure. The one I saw was definitely as big as that."

"Isn't it magnificent?" Ms. Bland asked. "Think that this work is almost four hundred years old, Mr. Dibble. Four centuries since Mercator sat down to create these drawings, imagining a world that he had never seen, putting on paper shorelines and borders that explorers from different countries reported back to the kings and queens who financed their voyages."

Booker didn't have to fake enthusiasm. He was so smart and such a curious guy that I could see he was able to completely put himself into his assignment.

"So Mercator was doing this in part from information of people who had traveled the world, mostly sailors and soldiers," Booker said, slowly turning the pages, "and in part . . . ?"

"From places he dreamed about," Ms. Bland said. "That's all it could have been in those early times. A man with a brilliant imagination. He created the first atlas—all European countries and principalities—

because there was a young prince who was planning to take his grand tour of the continent and wanted the most up-to-date vision of places that existed and what their boundaries were."

Ms. Bland kept an eagle eye on Booker's hand as he lifted each of the very colorful pages of the volume.

"But there were maps before Mercator," Booker said.

"Yes, indeed. He didn't invent mapmaking. His genius was connecting a map of country A to a map of the adjoining territory in country B. He bound them together for the first time, so that you could see the flow from border to border as you traveled, not just a series of independent maps that didn't appear to relate to one another."

Booker looked up at me and I mouthed two words to him. "Bad news?"

He got it. "By the way, Ms. Bland, what's the bad news?"

"Don't take any of this personally, Mr. Dibble, but there are two things. First is that I can only let you see one volume at a time."

He gave her that Dibble-dazzle smile. "That's no problem. I can't appreciate two at once," he said.

"Couldn't even turn the pages of these big guys at the same time."

"Very well," she said. "The other thing is that I have to sit here with you while you look at the Mercator. Watch you the entire time you have the book."

I almost interrupted with a *What? Not trust Booker Dibble?*

"But you seem to be here alone today," Booker said, much more diplomatically. He made it all about her and not about himself. A good trick for me to remember. "I can't possibly put you to that trouble."

"It's not just because you're a student, Mr. Dibble, or that you're young. I respect your intelligence, of course."

"Other people seem to be working from atlases and books, Ms. Bland," Booker said, keeping his cool. "There's no eagle eye on any of them."

"None of them have the Mercator," she said, reaching across to run her gloved fingertip along the top of the page it was opened to and stroking it lightly. "If I were to put this book up for sale tomorrow, Mr. Dibble, a rare book collector would probably offer me at least one million dollars for the two volumes."

"A million dollars!" Booker said, a little bit louder

than he'd meant to do, as his hands jumped from the atlas onto his lap. "You must be kidding?"

"It's no joke at all. That price at the very least."

"But—but I'm not going to walk out of here with it, Ms. Bland."

"Calm down, Mr. Dibble. I know you're not," she said. "One of us librarians sits with any scholar who looks at the Mercators. And with lots of other books that are as rare an antique as this, too. It's simply a rule."

Booker looked over at me and raised his eyebrows. I gestured with my hand that he should keep on turning pages.

"I wish I could put our most valuable books under bulletproof glass," the librarian said, pointing at the Hunt-Lenox Globe that Liza and I were gazing at. "But that doesn't work when there are pages that need to be turned."

"Do you think I'll get it dirty?" Booker asked. "Or that I'll accidentally tear a page and ruin its value?"

"Here's a sad fact, Mr. Dibble," she said, tapping her finger on the library table. "If you did decide to rip out a page of this atlas—and I'm not suggesting that you ever would—or perhaps even cut it out neatly with a pair of scissors, or a knife—"

I could hear Liza's intake of breath.

Ms. Bland looked up in our direction and scowled at Liza, then turned back to Booker. "You would accomplish two things if you did that."

Booker put his hands on the table beside the great atlas. "I'd ruin this beautiful work of art, Ms. Bland. I understand that. That's one thing."

"Correct. Its value would go from a million dollars to a fraction of that price," she said, "and it would break the heart of each of us who have cared for these precious treasures over the years."

"Yeah. I'm sure of that. But what else?"

"A person who steals a single page out of this book could sell it to a collector, or a dealer, as an individual map. Something rare that could be framed and hung in the private library of a person's home. An atlas sits closed on a shelf, while a Mercator map would dominate an entire wall. And without struggling to carry this volume out of the library and risk getting caught, a single page might sell for as much as half the entire book."

"Half a million dollars for one of these pages?" Booker asked, lifting the map of a section of China between his fingers.

"Indeed," Ms. Bland said. "Libraries have three

enemies, Mr. Dibble. We hold the history of the world within our doors, for all the public to see, but we fear three things."

"Fire," Booker said. "That would have to be one. And water. I know that floods from the beginning of time have been a terrible threat to all kinds of antiquities."

"Entirely right, young man. Entirely right. And then there are the third enemies, the horrible human beings, not accidents or forces of nature, but people who would deface books and destroy their value, all for personal profit," Ms. Bland said, shaking her gloved finger in front of his face. "Those terrible villains are the map thieves."

10

"Did you say 'thieves,' ma'am?" I said, swiveling from the globe to step toward the table. I dropped my tote from the seat to the floor and parked myself right next to Ms. Bland. "Where?"

I saw my opportunity to inject myself into the situation. Maybe we should just tell her what Liza saw yesterday.

She held her forefinger to her mouth and gave me that classic library *Sssssssh!*

"Thieves?" Liza followed my cue and rushed back to her seat next to Booker.

"Girls, girls, girls," Ms. Bland said. "Keep your voices down, please. There are absolutely no thieves in this library. I was just telling this young man a story."

"What's the story? May we hear it, too?" I asked as Booker kept turning pages. "What a beautiful book that is."

"Mercator's atlas," he said. "Shows every country in the world from the sixteenth century. Every one except Transylvania, if my teacher told me right."

I was kneeling on the chair and leaning in to look at the pages. "Transylvania fascinates me. It's where Count Dracula is from."

"Is there really a place called Transylvania?" Liza asked.

"Yes. It's part of Romania now," I said. I wanted the map librarian to warm up to us. I needed her to know that Booker wasn't the only smart one in the room. "There are supposed to be really strong magnetic fields in Transylvania, which gave lots of the people there extrasensory perception powers. That's part of the Dracula legend, anyway."

Miss Bland cocked her head and looked at me with a vague hint of a smile. "Very good, dear. Now, how would you happen to know that?"

"My school librarian. We studied the novel *Dracula* this year in class," I said. "We're going to do *Frankenstein* next. I just love my librarian."

"That's so good to hear. Your feelings for your

librarian, that is. Not necessarily her choice in fiction."

Okay, maybe it was a bit too smarmy of me, but Ms. Bland seemed to fall for it.

"But my friend and I like maps and globes even more than a lot of books," I said. "That's why we're studying the Hunt-Lenox."

I had Ms. Bland right where I wanted her. She was torn. She glanced longingly toward the tiny copper globe, clearly wanting to tell us more about it. Then she looked across at the Mercator and sat tight.

"Could you please give us some of the history of the globe?" I asked. "I'm sure you know everything."

"I can't right this minute. I'm helping Mr. Dibble with his project."

"Actually, Ms. Bland, why don't we take a break?" Booker said.

He closed the book and pushed it across the table to her waiting hands.

"Are you sure?" she asked. "I'll reshelve it for now and when you're ready to finish it and go on to the next half, I'll get them for you."

She picked up the heavy book and padded off again.

"How much of it did you get to go through?" I asked.

"I was trying to look for residue of tear marks, not study the maps, and it was hard to do that with her right by me the whole time," Booker said. "But there doesn't seem to be anything missing, as far as I got."

"Can't you finish it later?"

"Didn't you hear Ms. Bland? She claims nobody gets to use the Mercator without her standing guard. It would be way too lucky if the first book you picked was the one that had been defiled."

"Good point, Booker. Then let's not bother with the second volume. It's more important that we see the sign-in book," I said. "Make that happen, okay?"

"How do I do that?" Booker asked.

Liza was doing a Google search of the library collection. "Ask for something that's off-site, at another location," she said. "Like every other library, this one ran out of storage space. A lot of the books are kept off-site, or they even make you use digital copies."

"If it's off-site," I said, "you'll have to fill out a call slip and sign the book that we want to see. Good thinking, Liza. You can be my research assistant anytime."

"Assistant?"

"Partner. I meant to say partner."

Ms. Bland stopped to talk to a man who was waiting at the counter with a question. Then she headed back to us.

"Ask her for something by Thornton. Early seventeen hundreds," Liza said to Booker.

"You look so familiar to me," I said to Booker as she got close to the table. "What school do you go to?"

"Hunter," he said, biting his lip to hide a smile. "I think I've seen you before, too."

"Takes a good library to bring smart people together," Ms. Bland said. "Anything else you want today, Mr. Dibble?"

"Maybe something a little less pricey," he said. "Do you have anything by Thornton? Eighteenth century?"

"You're a quick study, young man."

"My classmates are very competitive. Got to stay on my toes."

"Most of the Thorntons we have are off-site."

Thumbs-up to Liza.

"If you don't mind filling out a call slip," she went on, "I'll order them in for you. Thornton's New England maps? New York?"

"New York would be great. I can come back later in the week."

Martha Bland turned away again, stopped at her desk to pick up some call slips, and then reached beneath it and pulled out what looked like a ledger.

"Should I tell her what I saw the tall man do?" Liza asked me.

I looked to Booker for guidance.

"What have you got to lose?" he asked.

"Well, if Ms. Bland doesn't believe Liza, or if she's offended that something bad happened to a library book right under her nose, she might throw us out of the building altogether, and then we'd be nowhere in all this. That's exactly why I didn't walk in the door and tell her about him first thing."

"Let's see how it feels when she comes back to us," Booker said.

"Wait for the right moment," I said. "We have no idea how long or short the list of people who requested books is for yesterday. In case she doesn't let us see it, let's get ready to split up all the names. Booker, you try to memorize the top third, Liza the middle, and I'll take the bottom."

"Done," Booker said.

"Call slips, young man," Ms. Bland said, seating

herself next to me. "Just fill them out with your personal contact information. I'll throw a wide net. Get you some other items that might interest you."

"Thanks very much."

She opened the ledger she had to a page that was place-marked with an index card. "You can take off your gloves, Mr. Dibble. It's just a musty old sign-in log. I need you to write your name, your e-mail address, and your school on today's page."

Booker removed his gloves and picked up the pencil.

I could see there were only seven or eight names on the page, under today's date. I needed to distract Ms. Bland so Booker could turn back a day.

"So isn't it really weird that this globe," I said, standing up and walking to the glass case, "doesn't have any outline of North America on it?"

She was on her feet again, joining me at the case.

"That's one of the things that makes it special," she said, describing to me the South American continent and some of the lands discovered by the Spanish and the Portuguese.

Booker had turned back the page and snapped a few photographs of it while I kept the librarian busy.

"We don't know who made this globe, dear, but he

obviously didn't believe in any of the Viking tales of discovery," she said with a smile. "Instead of America and Canada, there are just a few small islands here."

"And there's China, but he has it labeled East India," I said. "That's so odd."

"Very little was known of the Orient in 1512. Mostly just the tales of Marco Polo's travels," Ms. Bland said, looking over at Booker. "What are you searching for, Mr. Dibble?"

"I was curious about who else was looking at the Mercator this week. I feel like I'm in very special company."

"You certainly are. Yesterday I had a Harvard professor who spent most of the morning here. A history professor. And then a woman from England who's writing a book on the early Dutch explorers. The other librarian spent half an hour with her."

I walked around to stand next to Liza, peering into the ledger.

There were no times of day next to the list of names. It looked like there were more than fifteen of them, doing a quick scan.

"What are all the other books?" I asked. "Are any of them as valuable as the Mercator?"

Some people had signed in with first and last

names. I could eliminate the seven women without even blinking.

"All these books are rare, young lady. I don't think any would get quite the price of that atlas, but each one is here because it's part of a special collection."

I nudged Liza in the hip. It was time for her to tell Ms. Bland what she witnessed.

"I hope you don't think I'm rude, ma'am," she said. "But I was in here yesterday, taking notes about the globe for my school project, and I saw a man cut a page from one of your books."

"I don't believe that!" Ms. Bland responded sharply. "What book? Who was the man?"

"It had to be one of these guys," I said, pointing to the list in her ledger. "Not the earliest ones in the day, but somewhere after noon. If you give me these names and e-mail addresses, I can find out who did it."

"That's not possible. It's nonsense! I was in charge of the room all afternoon," she said, holding one hand to her heart as though that would slow down its beat. She glared at Liza again. "What book, I asked you? What happened to the page?"

"I—I don't know. The volume was very large and its cover was dark blue—"

"Most of the bindings are dark blue or black," she

said, snapping back at Liza. "Be more specific, if you can. And exactly what was on the page, please? Tell me that."

"I didn't see."

"Where did he put it? All the briefcases and bags are examined by security before you go out the front door."

"He didn't have a briefcase or bag. I didn't see it at all after he cut it."

"Then you're imagining things, young lady."

"I heard something, too, ma'am," Liza said. "I heard something metallic drop on the floor. It sounded like it could have been a small knife."

Ms. Bland reached into her pants pocket and removed a small metal case. My mother had one the same size. It was for folding reading glasses to keep in her small evening purse. The librarian dropped it on the floor. "Did it sound any different than that?"

"Pretty much like that. I'm not sure."

"Not sure? But you come in here accusing me of letting someone steal library property?"

That was a good reason for Ms. Bland not to believe Liza. Her own job would probably be at risk.

"I'm so sorry to upset you," Liza said. "It wasn't your fault."

"Don't apologize," the librarian said, grabbing the ledger from Booker.

"But the men who signed that list yesterday," I said, "it's not like you know them. You can't possibly assume that one of them wasn't up to any good here, when my friend was an eyewitness to the crime?"

"Innocent until proven guilty, young lady. Don't you know that's the law of the land?"

Few people knew it better than the kid of a prosecutor. "Beyond a reasonable doubt, Ms. Bland. Thanks for the reminder."

Liza and I picked up our things and dragged ourselves out of the elegantly decorated room. We were halfway down the hallway, waiting for Booker, so it didn't look like we had been in this together. No need to burn the nice lady.

"You called that one, Dev," he said. "She's taking the idea of a theft here way too personally."

"Cut to the chase, Booker, and pull up that snapshot you took. What names did you get?" I said. "I figure the Harvard professor and the English lady were closely watched, like Ms. Bland told you, because they were looking at the Mercator. You can take them off our list. As well as the six other women."

"Yeah. So there were eighteen names. Take away

those eight you've just suggested, and there are ten left," Booker said. "I've got the top six on the list. Two women and four men."

He read the men's names aloud to us, said he'd captured the e-mail addresses, too, and that three of the four had listed university affiliations while the other guy had left that space blank.

Booker forwarded the photo to both of us.

I had the bottom of the list. Five women and the last person who had signed in, probably too late in the day to be our suspect.

"What have you got, Liza?"

She opened the text and read from her portion of the list. "One woman only. Two high school kids, and three men, from some time in the middle of the day. One of the men owns a rare book and map store in Atlanta."

"He could be trouble," Booker said, "if he sells individual maps. I'll see whether his shop is online, or I can call them up."

"Another is a grad student at Columbia," Liza said. "And the third one, we can't really check him out because he didn't list a school or business or affiliation of any kind."

"Let's start with his name, Liza," I said. "I can't read his name. "

"That's just it, Dev. Here's this man, right in the middle of the pack—so maybe that places him in the map room while I was there—and Ms. Bland didn't even notice that he didn't write his name in the ledger."

"Well, what is this?" I was squinting at the letters on the small screen.

"Initials. Just three initials is all there is. Kind of sloppy handwriting. But it looks like the letters 'PJS.'"

"That's all?" I asked. "Not much to go on."

"PJS," Liza repeated. "And then an e-mail. It's 'BookBeast.' That's what he calls himself. BookBeast@xmail.com."

11

I couldn't wait to get through with dinner so that I could start my Internet search for all things related to the library and its visitors. Liza, my research partner, was having much too good a time talking with my mother and Natasha to hurry through the roast chicken and asparagus Natasha had prepared.

"I understand you saw Booker today," my mother said as I helped Natasha top off her ice-cream sundaes and serve them. "At the library."

My mother and his had been so close since their college days that it was impossible to put one over on them. Sometimes I think they communicate by brain waves, without talking, because they know each other inside and out. I just hadn't counted on them catching up before late evening. Must have been a slow day for both broken bones and the city's felons.

"I was going to tell you about it, Mom," I said. "Really, I was."

"Did you think it would go down better over dessert, instead of earlier in the meal?" she asked me with a smile.

"Sweeter this way," I said, kissing her on the cheek as I placed the ice cream in front of her.

"Somehow or other I thought I told you to leave the crime solving to the police."

"I thought that's what you said, too, Ms. Quick." Liza was definitely into scoring brownie points.

"I know you didn't like me chasing the man, Mom. I didn't think you'd mind, though, if we spent time doing research in the library. It's harmless."

"And you hooked Booker into your caper because?"

"Face it, Mom. You know that I am *nobody's* passport to cool," I said. "People trip over themselves to help Booker. This librarian today thought he was a junior or senior in high school."

"So did you solve the theft?" Natasha asked.

"Not even close," I said. "Here's the worst part. We decided to tell the librarian what Liza saw, but once we did that, the woman didn't believe her. She practically called Liza a liar."

I liked to separate the chocolate topping from the ice cream and save it for last.

"Try to eat that like a grown-up, darling," my mother said. She was great at diverting an issue and avoiding conflict. "By the way, I let Andy run your photos through the facial software program today."

"Anything at all?" I asked. That was my mother's nod to Liza that she understood that the story was true, even though I thought she was downplaying its significance to us.

"He told me the closest profile to the man you photographed was another species, Dev," my mother said, picking up her phone to read a text that had just come in. "A rodent of some kind, with a pointy chin and flared nostrils."

"That's ridiculous, Mom. Rodents don't wear glasses."

"Three blind mice, darling. Maybe they got their eyes examined after all these years." She pushed back from the table and stood up, patting me on the head and then texting a reply.

"Dishes or dog, Dev?" Natasha asked. "Pick your poison."

"Liza and I will take Asta out, okay?"

"Need any help with your homework before I go out?"

"Not tonight, thanks," I said.

"What are you doing this evening?" Liza asked.

"I'm going to the movies with a group of kids from my school," Natasha said.

Liza flashed me a look, like a secret grin, when Natasha answered.

"Liza's wondering if one of the kids is your boyfriend," I said, crouching down to put the leash on Asta. "She's completely boy crazy, Natasha. I'm missing the point of it, you know?"

"Plenty of time for all that," Natasha said.

"You've been hanging around my mother way too long," I said. "That's one of her favorite mottos."

"I don't think boys like me very much," Liza said.

"You're kidding. Booker thinks you're totally cool," I said. "I can just tell. He can't wait till we go to the park on Saturday night."

"He said that to you?" Liza's smile was so wide I could practically see the molars on which her braces were anchored. "Really?"

Booker didn't actually say Liza was the reason he was looking forward to our rendezvous. He loved picnics and was a big fan of Shakespeare, and the back-stage moment would suit him, too. But he did say he thought Liza's nerdiness made her almost cool.

"Really," I said. "Let's go, pooch."

It was still light outside. I figured that Asta had been cooped up all day, and I liked to let her lead us on a path that suited her curiosity. She sniffed along the sidewalk until we reached her favorite tree, then sniffed some more until she convinced us that she wanted to square the block looking for her pals.

Dogwalkers usually have a regular routine, my mother said. We were the exception because there seemed to be nothing routine about her professional life.

Natasha and I were out at different times of the day, so we recognized most of the canines and their families. Asta knew them all.

There was a pair of beagles approaching from the opposite direction. Their tails went berserk as Asta approached them. I greeted the humorless man who held their leashes in one hand and was texting with the other. He tugged them away from us and kept going. I much preferred his wife, who always stopped to chat with Asta and me.

"Don't take it personally," I said, bending to pat

my dog on the head. "We'll find you a buddy before we go upstairs."

I was trying to give quality time to my most loyal friend, Asta, and strategize about the next steps in the investigation, but Liza's mind was somewhere else.

"What are you going to wear to the picnic on Saturday?" Liza asked.

"You can't be serious."

Asta strained at the leash as we turned the corner. She spotted her favorite retriever half a block away. We broke into a trot and made directly for Ginger and the dogwalker who walked her in the afternoon and again in the evening.

The dogs circled each other with delight, yelping, while Asta rubbed herself against the taller girl's long legs, entangling the leashes.

"How are you doing in this heat, Devlin?" Amalie asked.

"Not so bad, Amalie. And you?"

She mopped her brow with a handkerchief. "Don't like it much."

"This is my friend Liza. She's visiting from Argentina."

"Pleased to meet you. You must be the only girls

left in this neighborhood," Amalie said. "It seems all the families around here have moved to the beach from this terrible heat."

"We're in summer school."

"Your mother works too hard," Amalie said. "She's in the newspapers every day. Tell her I said she needs to give herself a little holiday. And take you along."

I stroked Ginger's back and thanked Amalie as we walked on.

"She knows your mother?" Liza asked.

"She doesn't *know* know her. Everyone sees my mother in the neighborhood walking the dog with Sam late at night. Then they see her on the television news or in the papers, so they all feel familiar enough to pass along advice or comments. It's weird. There's a woman with a huge standard poodle who stopped me one day to tell me that my mom should wear more makeup when she's at a press conference."

Liza gasped. "What did you say?"

"I should have kept my yap shut, but I told her I didn't think the folks at the morgue who'd arranged the press release that day were worried about hair and makeup. At least, not for the living."

"The lady deserved that answer," Liza said.

We were three-quarters of the way home, and the sun had begun to drop behind the tall buildings on the west side of the park. Asta and I had greeted a lot of the locals and accomplished what we had set out to do when we left home.

"About the picnic," Liza said.

"Get over it, girl. I have no idea what I'll wear. Jeans. Shorts, if it's hot. Today's only Wednesday."

I could see our doorman standing under the awning of the building, about fifty feet away. He was in shirtsleeves and had taken off his hat, too. His back was to us and he was fanning himself with a rolled-up newspaper.

"Okay, then. Have you thought about what we're going to do tomorrow? About the case?"

"That depends on what happens tonight."

"Why tonight?"

"You'll see when we finish our homework. I've got a—"

"Devlin? Devlin Quick?"

It was a man's voice calling my name. I stopped short and looked over my shoulder. There was a guy across the street, a total stranger, raising his arm to wave at me.

"Aren't you Devlin Quick?" He stepped off the curb

but had to pause because a line of cars was passing between us.

Liza also turned when he called to me and seemed startled when she saw the man's face. She panicked, as though she recognized him, and started racing toward my building.

"C'mon, Dev. You need to run!" she said.

I had no idea what it was that spooked Liza, but she was moving like she'd seen a ghost. I leaned down to grab Asta and tucked her under my arm like I'd just caught a pass from Tom Brady and was making a run for the end zone.

"It's okay, Liza. I've got your back."

Liza had sprinted past the overheated doorman and was next to the elevator, doubled over trying to catch her breath.

I stood my ground at the front door. My mother would never forgive me if I let anyone frighten or harm Liza. Conduct unbecoming a police commissioner's daughter.

Within seconds, one of the cops in the patrol car who had seen us scrambling to get inside was right next to me.

"You two okay?" he asked. "What's the hurry here?"

Before I could give him an answer, Liza blurted out a response. "Don't let that man inside, Officer. He's after us!"

"Who is?" I started to ask her.

"He must be an accomplice to the map thief, Dev. A—a lookout or his partner in crime," Liza said. "I saw that guy in the library yesterday, too. I'm sure he's out to get us."

12

"It's all my fault, Blaine," Natasha said. "I'm so very sorry for upsetting Liza."

We were in the lobby of the building. Liza and I were sitting on the deflated cushions of the worn-out sofa, my mother and Natasha standing in front of us, with one of the officers by my mother's side.

The doorman was staring at something on the sidewalk, so I could only imagine that the second cop had our assailant—well, maybe the word "assailant" was an exaggeration—in handcuffs. Bystanders never tired of watching someone else's misfortune.

"Seems like a perfectly harmless situation," my mother said. "Tell me who he is, Natasha. He's a friend of yours?"

My mother probably wasn't happy about what had just happened, but it was so like her not to embarrass Natasha in front of all of us. She'd deal with that when they were alone.

Asta let out with a growl, low and long, in the direction of the front door.

"Asta's on our side, Mom," I said. "She wouldn't be growling if this whole thing was harmless."

"You've made her skittish, Dev. You girls panicked and that startled her. That's why she's growling."

"Don't blame the victim, Mom. Bad form."

"Fortunately you're not a victim. So don't exaggerate, dear."

"He's more like an acquaintance than a friend," Natasha said. "I've only known him a few weeks. He's one of the group going to the movies with me tonight. I can't imagine he meant any trouble."

"But—but he knew Dev's name," Liza said, looking up at my mother's stern face. "He called out her name from across the street. How would he know who she is?"

"I'm responsible for that," Natasha said. "I didn't want him coming to the apartment and starting with all that security stuff. I told him I'd meet him at the corner. He knows I live with you, Blaine. And with Dev."

"See what I mean, Liza?" I asked. "When I do get

old enough to have dates, I'll probably have to sneak off to coffee shops and secret passageways so the guys don't get frisked and fingerprinted."

"Don't let me ever hear the word 'sneak,' Dev," my mother said. "All your friends are welcome at our home. That's true for you, Natasha, just as it is for Dev. You know that."

"Yes, but I didn't want to bother introducing everyone in this little group," Natasha said. "I try not to talk about you, Blaine, but every time you're in the news, someone or other brings you up in conversation. Then there was that profile about you both in the article from Take Your Daughters to Work Day. What could be cooler than going to One PP as the commissioner's kid? Seems like everyone I know saw that piece."

"How did he know what Dev looked like?" Liza asked.

"There was a picture of her sitting at Blaine's desk in the centerfold of the magazine article," Natasha said, lowering her head. "I put it on my Facebook page, which was really stupid of me. I was just so proud of you both."

My mother put her arm around Natasha's shoulders. "That's entirely *my* fault. I thought Dev would get a kick out of having that photograph. I never imagined it would be part of the news article. I should have insisted they not use it."

"Don't forget you were walking Asta," Natasha said. "All my friends know about her, and they know where I live."

"Three solid clues," I said, nodding to myself. "Me—the kid in the photograph—with our pooch, and the building number printed on the side of the awning. Even a rookie could get lucky with those facts."

"What's his name, this friend of yours?" my mother asked Natasha.

"Jack. His name is Jack Williams."

"That's it," Liza said, clutching the arm of the sofa. "John Williams. Isn't Jack the nickname for John?"

"I—I'll have to ask him," Natasha said, looking puzzled.

"John Williams is the name of the Columbia graduate student who was signed into the Map Division at the library yesterday. His name was on the part of the list I had to memorize."

"I don't want to cause you any pain, Natasha," I said, "but your buddy may be a thief and a stalker, too."

She was ashen. "His big paper is about the New

York City grid," she said. "Of course he has to examine old maps. Let me go talk to him, please."

"What's the grid?" Liza asked me.

"It was the plan for the development of Manhattan's streets from, like, 1811—the single most important idea for the building of this city," I said to Liza before turning to Natasha. "You stay with Mom. I've got a lot of questions for Jack."

"No, *you* stay put, Dev," my mother said in her sternest command voice.

I really wanted to eyeball this guy to see whether I had noticed him lurking at the library, too. "But I know all about the grid, Mom. I can do this cross-examination. See what he was really up to."

"Everything you learned about the grid, you learned from me."

"I learned it from Sam, actually."

"May I come with you, Blaine?" Natasha asked.

"Best if you don't."

My mother uncrossed her arms, turned on her heel, and headed for the street. Even the nosy doorman stood at attention. I feared that Natasha's night at the movies was going down in flames once my mother got into her full-on prosecutorial mode.

"Sorry, Natasha," Liza said.

"You have nothing to be sorry about," she said, inching closer to the front door. "But what was it about Jack that sent you running for cover?"

"I don't know, Natasha," Liza said. "Maybe my nerves are just on edge because Dev and I are working this case. It's almost dark and along comes this guy who calls out her name. I recognized him right away, and I figured he might be part of this group of thieves."

Natasha turned to me. "You two need to take a break from what you're doing, Dev."

Fat chance of that, now that Liza made him as one of the library lurkers.

"Is he cuffed?" I asked her.

She stood inside the entrance and peeked out. "No."

"Has my mother started jabbing her finger at his chest yet? That's when I can tell she's really loaded for bear."

"No. She's letting him talk, actually."

"He was carrying a briefcase tonight, Liza, wasn't he?"

"He always carries a briefcase," Natasha said, before Liza could confirm what I remembered. "He's a grad student."

I was already pretty sure, from the way Liza reacted, that he's the accomplice to the tall man and spirited the stolen map out of the library for him.

"I hope you were going to the late show," I said. "You might be able to make it."

Natasha took a deep breath and kept up her stealth-like surveillance. "I couldn't sit still and concentrate on a movie. I'm too upset," she said. Then added, "Jack's a really good guy."

"Did Jack tell you he saw Dev at the library yesterday?" Liza asked.

"No. No, he didn't mention that," Natasha said.

"Was Jack at the library again today?"

"I don't think so. We were in class together this afternoon."

"You know my mom and Sam don't believe in coincidences," I said. "I mean, they don't believe in coincidences in solving crime."

"But coincidences happen," Natasha said. "Just because Jack was in the public library the same day Liza witnessed a theft doesn't mean he had anything to do with it. You girls are letting your imaginations get the better of your good sense."

Just then my mother stepped through the doorway into the lobby. She was followed by the second cop on the security detail—and by Jack Williams.

Liza gasped and grabbed my arm when she saw Jack come inside, just as I reflexively pulled Asta closer to me.

"Liza, Dev, let's not be rude," my mother said. "This is Natasha's friend, Jack Williams."

My mother expected a "how-do-you-do" from me but instead got just a frozen stare.

"I'd like to apologize for giving you a scare tonight, Dev. I shouldn't have called out your name on the street. I should have known better," he said. "Natasha's very loyal to her family, and I should have respected that."

"You're quite observant, Liza," my mother said, trying to take the attention off me and the pressure off this Jack Williams character. "You'll make a great investigator someday. That was indeed Jack at the library yesterday."

"I didn't know anything about a theft," he said, ignoring Liza and giving me his most earnest look. "I had my nose in my own research work, really."

"Why don't we let Jack and Natasha get on their way to meet their friends?" my mother said.

"Because I'm really curious about a few things, Mom. Can't Liza and I ask him some questions?"

"Sure," Jack said. "Ask me anything."

"Can we dump your briefcase?"

"What?" he asked, holding the case close to his chest.

"Dump it. Empty it out."

"Don't listen to her, Jack. She's just pushing my buttons," my mother said, shaking her finger at me. "Always remember to get your warrant first, Detective Quick. And that your evidence can't be stale. Most important when you're dealing with the public is to remember that the three words painted on the side of every NYPD patrol car are Courtesy, Professionalism, Respect."

"It's only been a little more than a day since Liza saw the theft, Mom. That's pretty fresh."

"So are you, Dev. Try courtesy. Jack's got an exam on Friday," my mother said. "Tonight's the one night he can relax with his friends before he goes into a final study lockdown. He's graciously agreed to come down to see Sergeant Tapply on Monday and go through everything we need to know about the library and the Map Division then."

"Monday?" I said, doing my best to sound completely exasperated. "It will be time to throw this whole thing over to the Cold Case Squad by then, Mom. The theft will be a week old."

My mother turned her back on Liza and me and walked Natasha and Jack to the door. I could see her squeeze Natasha's hand to assure her that she was totally fine with the situation.

"Don't let it get you down, Liza," I said. "You were great to recognize this guy tonight. If there's no break in an investigation, with any important kinds of crime, within the first forty-eight to seventy-two hours, it might as well be treated like ancient history."

"Well, I appreciate that your mother is taking it seriously enough to have this guy interviewed at the Puzzle Palace on Monday. At least she believes in us."

"Are you kidding? There's no time to be wasted. My mom just doesn't get the urgency of all this. I would hate for this map thief—or any of his cohorts—to become fugitives. By Monday, I expect that you, Booker, and I will have this whole caper solved."

13

"Are you sure you're done with your homework?" my mother asked when I pushed back from the dining room table. "Liza still seems to be going at it."

"We don't have all the same classes, Mom. I just knocked mine out faster," I said. "I'm going to read in my bedroom."

"Have you calmed down?" she asked me, reaching out for a hug. "Want a glass of warm milk to help you sleep?"

"I'm good. I wasn't really scared or anything."

"Don't ever be afraid to admit things frighten you, Dev. That's the healthy thing to do."

I hugged her as hard as I could. I hoped that she had someone she could confide in, too. I knew she hid all her fears from me.

I took my laptop to my room and set it up on my

bed. I e-mailed a couple of my friends to see what they were doing this week, brought Katie up to speed on the case, told Booker about the run-in with Jack Williams, and then got directly to work.

I created an xmail account in Liza's name, anticipating that I might be lucky enough to encounter the mysterious BookBeast at some point. Better to use her real name since she had ID to back it up, but I made up all her contact and other personal information. I didn't want the tall man—PJS, we thought—to have any way to actually find us.

I logged in to the private membership group I had joined the night before: the Latitude Society. I needed to catch up on the latest in exhibitions and news of rare map sightings and sales. I had to master the lingo and likings of the participants.

Not only had I created a new e-mail account for my membership account, but I had picked the perfect username. Most of the obvious ones were taken, like MapGuru and MercatorMiss. I channeled Liza's South American roots and called myself LatinaCarta, a South American woman who was into maps and charts.

"It's just me," Liza said as she opened the door to the bedroom and slipped inside. "Are you online?"

"Yes. I'm reading about the Latitude Society."

She put down her stack of books and climbed onto her bed.

"So what is it, exactly?"

"The home page describes the organization as a group devoted to the knowledge and preservation of antique maps," I said. "Let's see. There's a fund-raising part of it, to help libraries acquire expensive maps for their collections."

"Not us," Liza said.

"Certainly not. We meet twice a year at the NYPL," I said. "In November and in May."

"Not helpful."

"Smaller gatherings are encouraged when there are exhibits of special interest at other institutions. We have a quarterly newsletter, and we are encouraged to post interesting photographs of maps we own or see on kind of an internal Instagram. And bingo," I said with a burst of enthusiasm, "we blog!"

"Go for it," Liza said, clapping her hands.

I logged on to the private blog and entered my password. "Whoa," I said, "these dudes are serious."

"About what?"

"Wait a second. I'm scrolling down to look for obvious names."

"Like BookBeast?" Liza said.

"Yeah. Or someone with his same initials, PJS," I said. "Or maybe even Jack Williams."

Liza dropped her voice. "Are you also thinking he could be an accomplice in this?"

"Jack was in the library at the same time as the tall man, wasn't he? And he carries a briefcase," I said. "We can't rule him out just because he's Natasha's friend."

"I'm with you on that."

I was skimming some of the posts as I moved the cursor downward as fast as I could.

"Nothing yet?" Liza asked.

"No familiar names. But it looks like we missed a hot ticket event in Boston last month. Lots of chatter about how rare sea charts are because they weren't ever kept in libraries centuries ago like bound atlases were. They were used on sailing vessels to actually help captains navigate, so very few of them survived the salt sea spray and the shipwrecks."

"I didn't see anything on the sign-in page today about sea charts."

"I'm moving on from that topic," I said. "But this is promising. There was a cocktail party at the Vassar College library two weeks ago. Hosted by President

Catherine Hill, it says, to display some of the rarest maps in their collection, including a Mercator and an Ortelius, among a lot of others."

"What's so promising about that?" Liza asked.

"Remember when the tall man—the thief—beat us to the train at Grand Central Terminal?"

"Of course I do."

"The last stop on the train that he boarded was Poughkeepsie. That's the city where Vassar is."

Liza didn't bite without thinking. "But we saw him get on that train on Tuesday, two days ago, not two weeks. And there were lots of stops in between Manhattan and Poughkeepsie. It could be just a coincidence."

"I told you I don't credit coincidence in my sleuthing, Liza. I also don't ignore the baby steps it takes to put together a solution to a crime. It's a straight line from the map room on Fifth Avenue to Track 113 in the terminal to the Vassar College library, where there just happen to be Mercator atlases and other rare maps in the collection."

Liza was beginning to see the light. She nodded.

"Besides, I have someone to open the door to both libraries, which might catapult us right in to the information we need."

"Who's that?"

"My grandmother Louella Atwell. Vassar College, class of 1962."

"Amazing," Liza said. "But didn't you tell me your mother also went to Vassar? She's sitting right at the dining room table. We could just start by asking her."

"You've got to know your players, Liza," I said. "If I ask my mother one more question about the library or the map thief, I bet I'll be grounded for the foreseeable future. No Shakespeare in the Park. No Booker."

Liza frowned and twirled a few strands of her hair.

"My grandmother, on the other hand, she's the ticket, Liza. Lulu delights in teaching me how to take on the impossible."

14

"Last chance for milk and cookies," my mother said, opening the door and sticking her head inside. "Any takers?"

"No, thanks," I said as Liza shook her head. "We're good."

"How about lights-out in ten minutes? Finish up what you're doing, okay?" She walked over to kiss me good night.

"Deal," I said.

Then she walked to Liza's bed and kissed her on both cheeks. "See you in the morning."

Liza leaned forward to accept the embrace. "Yes, Ms. Quick. Thanks for everything."

I waited until the door closed and my mother's footsteps faded as she went down the hallway to her bedroom. Liza turned off her light, put on her pajamas, and slid under the covers.

"How's this, Liza? There's a meeting this Saturday at noon for Latitude Society members and their friends—that means you can bring me—at the Brooklyn library."

"The whole society?"

"No. Let me finish. It's a display of the sketches by Hernán Cortés from 1524."

"Cortés," Liza said, rolling her *r* as she propped her head up on the palm of her hand. "The conquistador who destroyed Tenochtitlán, the great Aztec capital."

"Yes. You should see the comments people are posting. This one could be lively. It's a small exhibition, and it's really just for people interested in early maps of the Americas."

"Like me."

"You bet. LatinaCarta is feeling the need to post something," I said, rubbing my fingers together. "I can just tell."

"What are they saying?"

"So what's on display is this rare book of sketches made by Cortés and his crew. It's the first map ever made of a North American city."

"That should be interesting."

"But then this guy starts ranting; his screen name is Montezuma."

"The Aztec leader captured and killed by Cortés," Liza said.

"Yes. So Montezuma writes in all caps, like he's screaming at the rest of us. He says it's not only the first map of Tenochtitlán, but it's also the last map. That after Cortés sketched the magnificent city, he burned it to the ground."

"*Exactamente*," Liza said. "I think I'm going to like Montezuma."

"Here's the thing. The map that's on display was stolen, Liza. It's only been recovered recently."

"Where was it stolen from?"

"From a book of sketches that was in the library at Harvard. It was sliced out of the volume by a knife of some sort," I said. "How's that for starters? It's been restored for this exhibition."

"Wow!" Liza said, sitting bolt upright. "A map thief at an important library, cutting rare sketches out of old books. That's the most exciting thing I've heard since we started on this, Dev. Your mom, Ms. Bland, Tapp, all the adults will have to take us seriously now."

"No kidding. This is big stuff," I said.

We both jumped off our beds and met in the middle to high-five each other.

"This is just what we needed, Liza."

I climbed back onto my bed.

"Now maybe people won't think I was making something up," Liza said. "What else are they talking about?"

"Some of the bloggers are saying how great it is that this was recovered. Wish they could be there to celebrate that aspect of things but they live too far away. Stuff like that," I said. "We've got to go to this on Saturday afternoon. Maybe it will draw the tall man back into the mix."

"Well, unless the librarian tells us what kind of books he was looking at on Tuesday, we don't have any idea if the Americas interest him. Besides, what do you intend to do if he does show up?"

"I'm sensing reluctance here, Liza. Just tell me if you're afraid."

I couldn't see her expression in the dark, from her side of the room, but she murmured a quiet no.

"The exhibit is about a very rare map, from an extremely early period of mapmaking, and it's got a whiff of scandal associated with it because it had once been stolen," I said. "Of course the tall man will come. It's got all the elements to attract him. It's like putting a bucket of treats under Asta's nose."

"Yes, but seriously, Dev, what would you do if you saw him again? What would you do if he walked into the Brooklyn library while we are there?"

"I guess I'd call Sam, or Tapp. Get them to send in an undercover to work with us."

"Is that enough?"

"We'll have Booker with us, I'm sure. I'll invite him."

Liza leaned back against her pillow. "That's a smart idea."

I went silent as I typed a message.

"What are you doing now?" Liza asked.

"Just introducing LatinaCarta to the group."

"What did you say to them?"

"I'm visiting from Buenos Aires and—"

"You didn't really do that, Dev, did you? I mean, it completely gives me away."

"No such thing. The foreign connection adds intrigue," I said. "I mean, if you talk to people, they're going to recognize your accent."

"You told me I hardly have an accent."

"It's a slight one. People are always friendlier when someone has come a long way to be with them. Besides, you're just going to be the daughter of LatinaCarta. We're too young for anyone to take us

- 136 -

seriously as members of a fancy map society. We just want to move around freely without posing an intellectual threat to anyone. Stealth-like observers."

"What else did you say?"

"That I'm, well, that you're especially interested in Dutch maps of the Americas."

"Why Dutch?"

"Because there are so many early mapmakers who were Dutch. It increases our chances if we cast a wide net," I said. "But I told them I really like things about Latin and South America, like the Hunt-Lenox Globe. And that I agree with what Montezuma said about Cortés—that he was a terrible person and they don't want to be involved honoring his work—which is why he and a lot of other bloggers are going to stay away from the library on Saturday."

"Well," Liza said, "those two about what kind of maps I like and agreeing with Montezuma about Cortés are true. I'm glad you said them."

"And I also wrote that unlike some of these Latitudes with attitudes, I find the idea of the theft fascinating," I said.

"You what?"

"I'm walking the walk, Liza. Talking the talk. It might take a thief to catch one. My exact words were, 'It's always such a temptation when I'm alone in a room with a spectacular map.'"

"You didn't really?"

"I did. I said I'd love to meet a map thief some day. I'd love to find out how one gets away with such a daring theft."

15

Sam was waiting for the three of us at the front door of our building. After the Jack Williams encounter last night, it was clear we'd be driven to school, even though it was such a short walk from home, so that our day would start calmly. I knew my mother wasn't worried about Jack because he was Natasha's friend, but she'd be sure, because of having Liza in her care, too, to double down on watching over us the morning after.

"Hey, Sam," I said. He high-fived me as I climbed into the back of the SUV.

"Devlin Quick," he said, closing the door behind me, "are you going to need your own police detail now?"

"That means Mom already told you about last night," I said. "Good to know she took that chance encounter seriously after all. And that you've run a record check on Jack Williams by now."

"Clean as a whistle."

"There's a first time for everyone, Sam."

Sam eyed me in the rearview mirror. I winked back at him.

"You look like you had a rough night, Liza," he said. "Didn't you sleep?"

"I, um, not really well, I guess."

My mother's head snapped around. Liza had dark circles under both eyes. "Were you that upset, Liza? You should have told me."

"It wasn't that, Ms. Quick. It really wasn't."

I knew what had kept Liza up was my plan for Saturday and crashing the exhibition at the Brooklyn library. I didn't want her to blow it for me at this point. "She's just a bit homesick."

Liza turned her head and grimaced. "I am not. Not at all."

"Let's call your mom right now," my mother said, handing Liza her cell phone.

"Really, it's not necessary. I think that would just alarm her at this hour."

"Then we'll do something fun tonight, okay? Let's go out to dinner. I'll check to see if I can get tickets to a Broadway show or something like that. Would you like that, girls?"

"Nothing special on my account," Liza said. "I'm really very happy doing what you all do ordinarily. I'm not homesick."

"I don't want to go to a show, Mom," I said. I couldn't imagine sitting through two long acts of some lame musical when I could be talking to my fellow Latitudians online. "Let's just pick a fun place to eat."

"That's a good idea," Liza said, trying to get back in my good graces.

"That's easy. What are you doing after school today?" my mother asked. "Natasha will be home studying whenever you get there."

"I thought I'd take Liza over to meet Lulu this afternoon."

My mother laughed. "That will make for a refreshing interlude, I promise you that."

"Just don't make the same mistake I did," Sam said, turning to look at us while he stopped at a traffic light. "Devlin was in one of her trickster phases when I first met Mrs. Atwell."

"Hey, I was only five or six years old at the time."

"No excuse, kid," Sam said to me, then explained

to Liza, "She told me to call her grandmother Lulu, just like she did. I almost had my head chewed off before I got two steps in the door."

"I'm the only one who can call her that," I said to Liza. "Kind of a special thing between us, since the time I started to talk and couldn't pronounce her name. She was trying to get me to call her Granny Louella, but all I could manage was Lulu. Otherwise she's pretty formal with people."

"Formal," my mother said, "and formidable."

"Zip it, Commissioner," Sam said to my mother. "Don't poison the well for Liza."

"You're right. That was rude of me. Louella Atwell is a remarkable woman, Liza. It's very cool for Dev to take you to meet her. She's got opinions about everything—very strong ones—and you should certainly get to know her."

"I'm looking forward to the visit," Liza said.

We had pulled up half a block short of the Ditch. I had worked out a deal with Mom and Sam that I didn't get dropped off right in front of the school, like some kindergarten kid. It was one less thing for the mean girls to make fun of.

"So I'll tell Natasha not to expect you till close to six?" my mother asked. "Then we'll all go out to dinner."

"Super," I said.

Sam checked the street for traffic. "The coast is clear, Devlin. Remember, kid, you're off duty today."

"Only if you come to dinner with us."

"When Sam or any other responsible adults tells you to do something," my mother said, "it's not your opportunity to strike a bargain, Dev. You *are* off duty. Got that?"

"Got it," I said, stepping out of the SUV. "What's your vote, Sam? Italian food or a good steak?"

"I think the commish needs some red meat, Devlin," Sam said, putting his sunglasses on. "We've got an overtime situation Saturday with a special noon session at the United Nations. The president may be flying in."

"Saturday? That's a bummer, Mom. We'll stay out of your hair," I said, resisting the strong impulse to do a fist pump. "You won't have to miss the picnic, will you?"

"I hope not. I don't think I'll make it to your swim practice in the morning, though. We start at the crack of dawn."

"No worries, Mom. There are no swim meets till the end of summer."

"Thanks for letting me off the hook, Dev," my

mother said, blowing kisses to both Liza and me. "Tell your grandmother the Red Sox will be at the stadium at the end of the month. I'll get the tickets if she buys the hot dogs."

I laughed as I turned away from my mother and Sam. "Those two are something to watch when they're in action," I said to Liza. "My mother is a die-hard Yankees fan. Lulu was raised in Boston and boos louder than anyone in the stadium. Ever hear of Boston Brahmins?"

"Brahmins?" Liza asked as we crossed the avenue. "They were the highest-ranking caste in an ancient Hindu society, weren't they?"

"Yeah. And for more than a century, it's what rich, elite Bostonians were called. And Lulu's one of them. She didn't exactly come over on the *Mayflower*, but that's probably just 'cause the staterooms weren't grand enough for her. That, and a few hundred years between the time it set sail and her birth."

"It sounds like your mom isn't so fond of your grandmother," Liza said.

I hesitated for a few seconds before I answered. "I doubt that they'd even talk to each other if it weren't for me," I said. "I'm sort of the glue that holds them together."

"Why don't they get along? Your grandmother's family was wealthy, right?" Liza said. "Is it because, well, if you don't mind my asking, your mother wasn't from that kind of background?"

"Oh, no. My mom grew up in a small town where her father was a firemen and her mother a nurse. Lulu thinks that firefighters and nurses are two categories of people who wake up each day just to do good in the world. She was fine with all that."

I held open the front door of the school and we walked inside. I did the mandatory bob in front of Wilhelmina Ditchley, gave it my best "We learn, we lead" in a firm voice, and then headed up the stairs.

"I'll tell you the rest later," I said as we took our places in the World Culture classroom.

I checked my iPad to see whether anyone from the Latitude Society had responded to my blog entry. I replied to Booker, who was shocked to hear about our encounter with Jack Williams, and then I got back to note taking for class.

The second session was down the hall, in a much larger room, where we spent ninety minutes reliving the fall of the Bastille.

As the class ended, the teacher planted herself in

front of me. "You don't seem yourself today, Dev. You were unusually quiet. Are you all right?"

"Yes, ma'am. I'm fine, thank you."

"You seem distracted?"

"No, no, I was paying close attention. It's just such, such a sobering moment in history. All those beheadings, and people putting the governor's head on a spike."

"On a pike, Dev," she said, frowning at me. "I said it's a pike. It's a medieval weapon, different from a spike."

"Sorry," I said, looking down to straighten my pile of books. I thought pike was a kind of fish and a spike was something with a dangerous pointy tip. Like my mother tells me, pay attention in school and you can learn something new every day.

"Dev?"

"I misheard you," I said. Direct eye contact with her was difficult, since I'd actually been Googling subway directions to the Brooklyn Central Library when the Bastille was being stormed a few minutes earlier. "The man's head was on a pike. Now I know that."

"Do you remember the governor's name?"

"I'm afraid that I don't."

The frown deepened. "And the reason for the actual assault on the old prison . . . ?"

"Was because of the abuses of the monarchy," I said, parroting the words she had used. "The flashpoint of the revolution is what you called it."

"Very good, Dev. At least you were listening to me yesterday."

"I was totally concentrating on the lesson today, too."

"Then how many prisoners were actually inside the Bastille at the time it fell?" she asked. She was gloating now, sure she had landed the final blow, the *coup de grace*, which would cause her to move my seat to the front row tomorrow and allow her to assign me extra readings over the weekend.

I lifted my head, about to acknowledge defeat. But there was my loyal friend Liza, just behind the teacher's shoulder, holding her fingers in the air.

"Seven. I believe that's the number you told us. Seven prisoners. All common criminals"—that's the part I had heard clearly—"not political powers."

Liza's thumbs-up was an antidote to the teacher's sour expression.

"I'm so pleased you were able to focus, despite the difficult subject matter. There's always been a bit of revolutionary spirit in you, Dev. But you seemed miles away today."

"Closer than you'd think, ma'am." Brooklyn's Central Library was an easier trip than I had guessed.

"Good. You can go on to your next class now. See you in the morning."

I stood up and thanked her for such an enlightening lesson.

Liza was already walking in the opposite direction. She turned her head, and I waved at her as I walked toward the school library. I ducked into the girls' bathroom to call my grandmother—no cell phone use allowed at the Ditch, of course—and told her housekeeper that Liza and I would like to come to lunch.

I was the last one into Miss Shorey's classroom. I apologized for holding her up as she closed the door behind me.

The eight of us were gathered around two long tables in the center of the room. "Before we begin our conversation," the librarian said in her soft voice, "something Dev and I have been talking about this week sparked an idea."

All heads turned in my direction and I slunk down in my chair, fearing the disapproving glances of my peers.

Miss Shorey walked to her desk. "Just because you like to read so much, Dev," the girl closest to me said, "doesn't mean I need another assignment this weekend. Thanks a bunch. Not."

"I know that three of you will be absent tomorrow," the teacher said. There was always a drop-off in Friday numbers for the kids who had somewhere to go on weekends. "I thought, since we'll only be five, that it would be fun to have a field trip for the afternoon."

I smiled and straightened up. Best of all worlds. No more homework for the complainers, and a chance to be out of this building on a bright summer day.

"There are so many wonderful things to see that can give you a tangible connection to the books we're reading and to the men and women who wrote them," Miss Shorey said. "I thought we might go to the New York Public Library and explore some of the treasures there."

It suddenly felt like someone was break-dancing in my stomach. No way I could go to the library and chance a run-in with Ms. Bland, who might complain about me to Miss Shorey. Or risk an encounter with the tall man without Liza and Booker at my side.

She reached into her desk drawer and came up

with a handful of papers. "I'll need you each to have a parent sign a permission slip, of course."

Some girls had forged their mothers' signatures on report cards and would do the same for this kind of thing. That was one felony beyond my imagination, but I couldn't imagine asking the commissioner to authorize this particular trip.

"You look disappointed, Dev," Miss Shorey said.

Again all the heads turned.

"Not at all, Miss Shorey. I—I just want my project for World Culture to be a surprise," I said. Best excuse I could muster was blaming Dickens's poor old stuffed cat's paw for my reluctance to revisit the scene of the crime. "A couple of these girls are in my World Culture class, too, and it would just spoil it for each of us."

"Very thoughtful of you, Dev. You can each tell me what your particular object is," she said, nodding over to me, "so that I can arrange that they don't have it on display tomorrow. I don't plan to spoil your surprises. Besides, there are so many special places to see in that library. There's a conservation laboratory where ancient books are restored, there's a reading room larger than a football field, and there's the Map

Division, which has some of the rarest maps and charts in the world."

The break-dancer rattling my insides just did a backflip and landed in a split. The Map Division was one place I did not want to visit on a class trip this week.

"Will that bring back your smile, Dev?"

"It's a great idea, Miss Shorey," I said, giving her my best grin. A fiblet, to be certain, but I couldn't spoil her generous gesture. "A really great idea."

16

"Help me figure a way out of Miss Shorey's field trip," I said to Liza, stuffing the permission slip into my pocket. "My mother will assume I put her up to this."

"You'll think of something, Dev. You always seem to."

It was a very long walk from East End Avenue, where the Ditchley School had been situated since its founding nearly a century ago, to the Fifth Avenue apartment that had been my grandmother's home since her marriage to Henry Atwell when she was twenty-eight years old.

"Tell me more about your grandmother," Liza said.

"Everybody should have a Lulu in her life. I know you don't have either of your grandmothers alive, so

I'm happy to share her with you," I said. "What do you want to know?"

"Well, her story, I guess."

"Lulu's family were Boston Peabodys. You'd need a family tree with more limbs than you could count to trace them back to their roots. Her grandfather worked with the great American industrialist Andrew Carnegie. That's what created the family fortune, and also inspired the kind of philanthropy that she believes in."

"I don't know about Andrew Carnegie," Liza said.

"He was a totally self-made immigrant who worked his way to the top in the steel business. Billions of dollars, most of which he tried to give away before he died. Carnegie gave away enough money to build more than two thousand public libraries all across America."

"That's amazing. And Henry Atwell, what was his fortune?"

"He didn't have one. Lulu was looking for two qualities in a prospective husband: brilliance and a sense of humor. Hit the mark on both.

"She was a child of the sixties, Liza. She rallied for the Equal Rights Amendment, she protested against the war in Vietnam, and she marched from Selma to Montgomery for the Voting Rights Movement. That's where she met my grandfather."

"Bloody Sunday?" Liza asked, referring to the dreadful day in 1965 when Alabama state troopers attacked the unarmed marchers.

"No. That's the day that caused her to join the second and third marches. Henry was a journalist covering all of them. He actually won a Pulitzer Prize for his articles. His father was a shoemaker in a small Midwestern mill town, but Grandpa Henry won a full scholarship to Yale. He used to tell me he fell in love with Lulu when he picked her up off the ground that day—he'd never laid eyes on her before—after she was hit with tear gas in Montgomery. He'd laugh and say that the moment he met her was the only time he'd ever see her cry," I said. "That was true until the day she got the news my father had been killed."

Liza had no response. I hadn't meant to be dramatic, but that story was the truth.

"She sounds tough."

"It's in her genes, she says. Both her parents were activists, too, and interested in good works. They never let her be a debutante," I said. "They insisted she have purpose in her life and that she stand for something."

"That's so interesting," Liza said.

"Then there's her education at Vassar. It was a women's college when Lulu went there. She says that's what made her such an independent spirit."

"Was Vassar still a women's college when your mother attended?"

"No. It went coed in the 1970s. Sort of funny because my mom claims that she gained most of her independent thinking at Vassar, too. Going head-to-head with so many smart guys, as well as other women."

"But if they're so much alike, Dev, why don't they get along?"

We were crossing Park Avenue on our trek to the heart of the fanciest residential part of Manhattan. We were stuck between lights on the median, and I couldn't avoid the conversation.

"It's all about my father, Liza," I said. "Everything important in my life seems to be about him."

"I'm so sorry, Dev."

"Don't be sorry. It's nobody's fault." Nobody except the person who killed him, is how I looked at it. "He was born a year after Lulu and Grandpa Henry Atwell married."

"Devlin. So your father was Devlin Atwell," Liza said, as though a light had suddenly switched on in her brain. "But you're Devlin Quick."

"That's a major part of the problem right there," I said, scooting across the avenue to beat a trio of oncoming cabs. "My mother was very stubborn, especially since I was born after my father's death. She figured it would just be the two of us, on our own. The two of us making our own way in the world. She wanted me to be a Quick, just like she was. She insisted that I carry her name."

Liza had no comment.

"She also refused my grandmother's offer to have us both move in with her and raise me there."

"But why?"

"You're about to see why. Because Lulu lives in a Fifth Avenue penthouse that looks like an annex of Buckingham Palace. She's got a housekeeper and a chef and a butler. My mother wanted none of that for me. I'm *her* child, and I would always be known as her child, since I didn't have a father. So she decided I might as well have her name and live the life she was living."

"And your grandparents resented that," Liza said.

"Yeah. My mom says they didn't understand just how deep her grief went, and that she wanted to figure out her own way to cope with it. They underestimated her strength. I know they meant well, but it was apparently quite a scene at the time."

"She won't take money from your grandmother, either?" Liza said, craning her neck to look up at the grand entrance to Lulu's building.

"How do you do, Miss Quick?" the doorman said to me. His uniform was as well-tailored as a designer suit. "Shall I announce you?"

"Please do, thanks," I said, then continued to answer Liza. "I think my father's inheritance is in a trust for me. My mother refuses to discuss that. She and I live entirely on her salary. She was insistent on that, too. The only exception is that Lulu pays my tuition at the Ditch, 'cause my mother agrees it's the best school in the city."

"That looks like a Van Gogh," Liza said, studying the large painting on the wall of the lobby as we waited for the elevator.

"You even know a lot about art, Liza. That's cool," I said. "It's actually a real Van Gogh."

"Are you kidding?"

"Nope. Lulu ran out of wall space upstairs, but she wasn't quite ready to give it over to the museum yet," I said. "She's really something."

The door opened and the white-gloved elevator man welcomed us on and pressed the PH button that would take us up to the top floor. "Good to see you, Miss Quick. You'll be making your grandmother's day, won't you now?"

"That all depends on whether I remember my manners, I think."

"Well, the entire building staff will know about it if you don't, young lady. You're the apple of her eye."

"Then I'll be on my best behavior, just for you," I said, turning back to my friend. "By the way, Liza, I know you've got a really intense streak of curiosity, which I appreciate. But do not go asking Lulu if she has a boyfriend, like you do everyone else."

I never expected Lulu to be standing on the landing when the elevator doors opened. It was usually the housekeeper who let me in.

"Why is that, Devlin?" Lulu asked as I stepped toward her. "Would it shock you to think I have a suitor at this age?"

She practically smothered me in an embrace. I hugged her back, then reached up and kissed her cheek.

"Not at all, Lulu. It's just that the last guy dropped dead on you at the Metropolitan Opera House in the middle of the second act of *Othello*," I said. "Take a breather, why don't you?"

"Gentlemen keep me engaged in the world, my darling. That one had a weak constitution, sad to say. A Wagnerian opera might kill a man, but I didn't think this one could. Now, make your proper introductions."

I presented Liza to my grandmother, a plump woman about two inches taller than I was. Lulu had deep blue eyes, hair that was as white as new-fallen snow, and skin that never wrinkled as she aged.

"Delighted to meet you, Liza," my grandmother said. "Devlin tells me you're from Argentina. I've been there many times throughout my life, greeted with great hospitality, so I want you to feel very much at home while you're in this country."

Lulu took off chattering in Spanish—she spoke French and Italian, too—although the only thing I was able to understand was her admiration as a young girl for Eva Perón because of her struggle for women's suffrage.

She and Liza were walking into the living room, with its breathtaking views of Central Park. Liza was as happy as I'd seen her since the day we'd met as she responded to all of Lulu's questions.

"I understand I'm to feed you girls," she said, ringing a small silver bell on the end table next to her sofa. "Let's see if lunch is ready. Then perhaps Devlin will tell me what prompted this visit."

I flopped down on the oversized chintz cushion of the sofa. My feet almost reached the floor, which meant that I had grown a bit in the last month. "I've got no agenda, Lu. I wanted Liza to meet the world's greatest granny. Simple as that."

"What do you take me for, Devlin? I know I can have the cook whip up a wicked PB&J sandwich for you on a moment's notice, my dear, but you've got way too many things to do on a beautiful summer afternoon to drop by just to humor me."

"I'm starving to death," I said. "Why don't you feed us first?"

The cook, Bridey, appeared in the archway in response to the bell call. "Welcome home, Devlin," she said, blowing me a kiss. "Luncheon is served, Mrs. Atwell."

"I always know when you're in desperate need of an ally or a partner in crime, Devlin Quick," Lulu said, patting me on the head as she led the way into the dining room. "I must teach you to be more subtle in your approach, dear. As it is, I can tell when you've got something up your sleeve. You might as well let your secret out of hiding."

17

"What are you girls working on in summer school?" my grandmother asked. "I'm told the Ditchley has a very ambitious program."

Bridey had set a small round table for us against the window in the dining room, also fronting Central Park, but far more intimate than the long banquet table that held twenty-four of us at Thanksgiving and Christmas, when my relatives came to town.

I let Liza describe the courses she was taking while I tried to think of the best approach to enlisting Lulu in our crime-solving caper.

"Thank you," I said to Bridey as she set a bowl of soup in front of me.

"What's our starter?" Lulu asked.

"It's a cold avocado soup, ma'am. Devlin's favorite.

And I've added some cucumbers and cherry tomatoes for color."

"Very kind of you, indeed," my grandmother said. "And on very short notice. Do go on, Liza."

I loved Bridey's soup but was still what Lulu referred to as a finicky eater. I tried to fish out the annoying cucumber slices, spearing them with my fork as though it were a pike, while Liza engaged her in conversation, but she caught me out of the corner of her eye.

"Your mother's right about one thing, Devlin. Your table manners would have people think you were raised in a barnyard."

"Sorry, Lu."

"Eat the food in front of you; don't play with it. It looks like you're growing some muscles on that slim frame."

"You know I need that for my swimming. I've got practice at nine o'clock on Saturday morning. Would you like to come watch?"

"I'd adore that, Devlin. You know I would," Lulu said, turning to Liza, who had perfect manners to match the perfect posture as she raised the soup spoon to her mouth. Looking at her made me sit up straighter without even thinking about it.

"My grandmother was on her swim team, too," I said to Liza. "All through high school and even at Vassar. Isn't that fun? It's one of the reasons I enjoy racing. I try to imagine that Lulu's in the next lane and I'm determined to beat her. I wish I could time travel back and dive in together with her to see who would win."

"Yes," Lulu said, "we're both champions at the Australian crawl. Not any longer for me, of course, but I love to root for Devlin. She's got a better turn off the wall than I ever did, but my crawl stroke was so much cleaner than hers. You need to keep working on that, dear, don't you?"

"It's called freestyle now, Lu," I said. "No one calls it the crawl anymore."

"*Plus ça change, plus c'est la même chose*, my dear. Do you speak French, Liza?"

"I do a bit. 'The more things change, the more they stay the same,' isn't that the translation?"

"Good for you," Lulu said. "You see, Devlin? You really need to start taking foreign languages. It so increases your reach, now that the world is shrinking. Besides, darling, I know the stroke is called freestyle now. It's just that I crawled for so long that some habits are hard to change."

She asked Liza about her athletic ability and the two discussed soccer, while I continued to noodle through the best approach to her.

"It's good for everyone to have a sport, girls," Lulu said. "The exercise, the competition, the sportsmanship and camaraderie with your teammates. All valuable assets. Builds character for you."

"So you'll come on Saturday to watch me?"

"Another time, Devlin. I'd so like to do it, but I'm going to stay with friends in East Hampton this weekend. Will that be a terrible disappointment to you?"

I got up from my seat and wrapped my arms around my grandmother from behind as Bridey cleared the soup dish and replaced it with my sandwich. "You could never disappoint me, Lu. You're the only guardian angel I've got. You're the best."

"I can see we're getting closer to the real reason for your visit, darling." Lulu cut me off like a stroke of the guillotine. "Spare me the flattery, Devlin, and tell me what has you stumped."

I had taken my first bite of the peanut butter and jelly sandwich, wickedly good, as she was quick to say, because she used a divine jelly preserve she had shipped to her twice a year from the South of France.

The peanut butter was stuck to the top of my mouth like glue. I couldn't speak. At home, I could have scooped it out with my finger, and my mother would have simply shaken her head, but finger scooping was forbidden on Lulu's territory. I motioned to Liza to begin.

"I witnessed a theft, Mrs. Atwell," she said. "I saw a man cut a page out of a valuable book at the New York Public Library."

"Heavens!" my grandmother said, clutching one hand to her breast. She, of course, had cut her sandwich into half-inch squares and was eating bite-size pieces in a thoroughly adult way so that there was no accumulated mass to stick to her palate. I had so much yet to learn about life.

Liza went on with her narrative. I watched Lulu's face while Liza talked. She was the first adult to whom we'd told the story who found it thoroughly credible and completely outrageous.

"What's the commissioner of police doing about this crime?" she asked me. "What does she say?"

I hadn't expected that question. I had no intention of setting my mother against my grandmother.

"She's taking it seriously, Lulu," I said, treading water cautiously. "My mother has a few things on

her plate that appear to be more urgent, like terrorists and murderers and all that. I can't blame her a
bit."

"Has she put Dick Tracy in charge of the investigation?" she said, smirking at me.

"His name is Sam Cody, Lulu. I know you know
that. And yes, he's been helpful, too." I think my
grandmother was jealous of the time that Sam spent
with my mother, and the closeness of their relationship.

"Then what can you possibly need from me?"

"Nobody on this planet knows libraries as well
as you do, Lu. I'd like you to help us think of a way
to catch this—I mean to help the police catch this
man," I said. "He may even have accomplices. Have
you ever heard of a map thief before?"

Louella Atwell nodded her head but was slow to
answer. "I have. Certainly I have."

"Where?"

"In the very same room where Liza witnessed
this terrible act. More than a decade ago, a man was
caught who'd gone to all the great research libraries
up and down the East Coast. Caught at Yale University, finally. But he left his mark here in New York,
too."

"Well, there's another thing you ought to know, Lulu," I said. "We followed him from the library—"

"You did *what*?"

"She means that before we turned the matter over to the NYPD, Mrs. Atwell," Liza said, "we followed the man to Grand Central Terminal and saw him get on a train that—"

I had to jump in at this moment. Point of pride, I guess, because of Lulu's connection to Vassar College. "A train that was headed for Poughkeepsie. So I'm sorry that you're upset about us following the man but—"

"Upset? I'm not the least bit upset, Devlin. Done with aplomb, I would say quite heartily."

"I don't know that word," Liza said. "'Aplomb.'"

I smiled at Lulu while I answered Liza. "Sort of means self-confidence, with assurance. My grandmother's not criticizing what we did, like everyone else has. She's paying us a compliment."

Lulu dabbed at her mouth with her cloth napkin. "Moxie, young ladies. I like that you've got moxie."

"There's more, Lu," I said, barely able to contain my enthusiasm. "We believe the thief may have something to do with Vassar."

"Really? How did you reach that conclusion?"

"There was something online about an exhibition in the college library, and a cocktail reception that was held there two weeks ago. President Hill hosted the party and there were rare maps by Mercator and Ortelius on display."

"You think your thief might have been in attendance?" my grandmother asked.

"It's not just a wild guess, Lu. He got on a train bound for Poughkeepsie the other day. It's just possible that he has a connection to the school, or that he went to the reception."

Louella Atwell was on her feet. "Is your mother following this lead, too?"

I looked away from her, staring out instead at the horse-drawn carriages winding their way through the park paths below us. "She doesn't have any jurisdiction in Poughkeepsie."

There was a small salon between the dining and living rooms where Lulu kept a writing desk and an old-fashioned landline telephone. "Well, I still do," she said, planting herself firmly in the upholstered chair.

"Do what?"

"Have jurisdiction of some sort in Poughkeepsie, Devlin. The college is courting me for my collection of paintings by the Hudson River School artists."

She opened her address book—no digital contact list for Louella—and found the number she wanted to dial. "Good afternoon," she said to the person who answered on the other end. "This is Louella Atwell calling for President Hill."

There was a short pause.

"I'll hold," my grandmother said. "No, I don't care how long I'll have to wait. Please tell her Louella Atwell again, won't you?"

Then she looked back at the two of us. "Do you know anything about your thief? Do you have a name, or a good description?"

I gave her the bits and pieces we had, which she confirmed were woefully inadequate.

"We think his initials might be PJS," Liza said. "Or maybe he's Jack Williams."

My grandmother held up her hand to quiet us. "Good afternoon, Ms. Hill. Yes, this is Louella. I'm close to a decision on my paintings, but I'm curious about whether you can help me with some information about a reception you held at the library two weeks ago."

I was so excited that Lulu might actually move us closer to a solution that I was practically quivering.

My fingers on both hands were crossed, and I stuck them under my knees to keep them still.

Lulu put her hand over the mouthpiece of the phone after giving the president the information she had, and requesting a guest list of the party. "Devlin, darling, stop biting your lip. You're going to put a hole right through it."

"Does President Hill have names, Lu?"

"She's going to check for me."

My grandmother perked up and held the phone closer to her ear, repeating what she heard as she wrote on a notepad in front of her.

"Five folks from the administration," Lulu said. "You and the development office. And only sixteen guests. A rather poor showing, don't you think, Ms. Hill?"

I winced at my grandmother's frank appraisal.

"I see," she went on. "Late notice. Thunderstorms all day. I see, I see. Surely a tall young scholarly-looking gentleman with spectacles would have been memorable among all those rich old goats gawking at your maps, don't you think?"

Dr. Hill must have responded.

"The sooner you get me the registration list the better," my grandmother said. "I understand that you're certain you saw no one of that appearance, but a list of names would be most helpful."

Lulu replaced the phone in its cradle. "Now, there's a brilliant woman," she said. "And a terrific position to aspire to, girls. Nothing more challenging in this day and age than to be a college president. The economics of education, the importance of diversity on campus, safety issues—not to mention actually teaching students something amidst all this turmoil."

She pushed back from the writing table and stood up. "Do I need a sweater over my shoulders, Devlin? Or is it terribly hot outside?"

"It's warm, Lulu," I said. "Are you going somewhere?"

"Of course I am. The three of us are, girls. We're going to pay a visit to Ms. Bland."

Another heart-stopper.

"But, Lulu, Liza and I can't go back to the public library." All roads seemed to be leading me there, I thought. "Ms. Bland got mad at us yesterday. We don't want her to lose her job because of this."

"You can't keep the truth hidden, Devlin," my grandmother said. "You must always fight for what is true. The only person with something to fear, girls, is the map thief. He's the only one who ought to be afraid right now."

My grandmother picked up her pocketbook and continued her strides to the front door. If she was right about that, then why was I so frightened?

18

The three of us Ubered down Fifth Avenue toward the library. I texted Booker as fast as I could. Where R U now? Lulu taking us to Library. B there.

The usual traffic that jammed the Fifty-Seventh Street intersection slowed us down. It was fifteen minutes before the driver deposited us at the bottom of the steps in front of the friendly lions.

"Lulu's a trustee of the New York Public Library," I whispered to Liza. "Expect fireworks."

"Let me take your arm on these stairs," my grandmother said to Liza. "This is my favorite institution in the City of New York. I'm so glad you've been studying here."

We made the climb slowly as Lulu caught her breath on the wide plaza halfway up. "Privilege," she said to both us, "privilege without purpose is meaningless. I've tried to drum that into Devlin's brain since she was a toddler."

"I get it, Lu. I really do."

"I was born to great privilege, Liza," she went on, "and made to understand how important it is to *stand* for something. To do something for the greater good. As well as to do it quietly."

She pushed against the heavy door of the library entrance. Liza and I followed her inside and took giant steps to keep up with her as she headed directly down the long corridor to the right, to the Map Division at the very end of the hall.

I ran a few steps ahead and pulled open the door to the room. Six or seven people were scattered at the rectangular tables in front of us. No one looked up as we walked in.

There was no one seated at the librarians' desk, but that was exactly where Lulu was going.

"See that man at the table against the window?" Liza asked. "The guy who just stood up?"

"Yes," I said.

"He was here on Tuesday, too. I remember his shiny forehead and that tie with the design of books all over it."

The man looked older than my mom but younger than Lulu. He had opened a small shopping bag and placed his notepad inside it. Then he picked up the volume he'd been working with in his gloved hands and walked to my grandmother's side, smiling at her as he placed the book on the desk.

He cupped his hands over his mouth, directing his words to someone out of sight behind a bookshelf. "Good-bye till next time, Ms. Bland," he said. "Y'all stay cool this summer."

The man had a strong Southern accent. I wondered whether he could be the owner of the rare bookstore in Atlanta, one of the visitors who had logged into this division on Tuesday, when the theft occurred. Of all the days for Booker not to respond to my text for backup. I needed his moral support, his calm presence, and his ability to follow this dude while I stayed close to Lulu.

By the time Ms. Bland appeared from behind the shelves, the man had left the room. The last person she expected to see at her desk, or so it seemed from the expression on her face, was my grandmother.

"Why, Louella Atwell," she said, practically gasping for air. "No one told me you were coming today."

"I'm under the impression, my dear woman, that

this is a public library. I wasn't aware that appointments were required."

"Certainly not," Ms. Bland said. "You're welcome anytime."

Her head was bouncing back and forth between Liza and me.

"I think you've had the pleasure of meeting my granddaughter, Ms. Bland. This is Devlin Quick. As in quick like a fox. And this is our dear friend Liza. Liza de Lucena, visiting from Argentina."

"Your granddaughter, is it?" Ms. Bland said, tapping her fingers nervously on the countertop. "How lucky you are. And what brings you all here today?"

"It's my understanding that these young ladies told you that they had witnessed a crime."

Ms. Bland didn't speak.

"There's no need for you to be nervous, my good woman. They didn't point a finger in your direction," my grandmother said, "and we all know what an asset to the institution you are."

"Kind of you to say, Mrs. Atwell, but—"

"But what, Ms. Bland? Surely you trust my granddaughter?"

"Yes," she said meekly. "Of course I do. But she's a child, really, and I'm not certain we can rely—"

"A child?" I blurted out. "I'm twelve years old. I'd hardly call that—"

"Manners, Devlin," Lulu said, her forefinger to her lips to silence me, as she kept her eyes directed at Ms. Bland. "These are extremely intelligent young ladies. They are Ditchley girls."

Ms. Bland wasn't much moved by that fact, although the mothers of half the city's pre-K kids would have been weak-kneed at the thought their daughters might one day test into the famous school.

"I'm sure they're very capable, Mrs. Atwell. And as you well know, I've had experience with map thieves before. I feared, because of their tender age and lack of, well, worldly experience, these two observers might have been confused about what they thought they saw."

"Devlin Quick, I'll have you know," my grandmother said, "already has impeccable credentials as a sleuth. She has solved mysterious disappearances from the locker of a classmate at school, put a halt to the cyberbullying of a friend's younger sister, and safely recovered a neighbor's gerbil that had gone missing for days. Devlin Quick knows a crime when she sees it."

"Remarkable," Ms. Bland said, giving me one of those fake smiles that adults often bestow on kids they don't really like. "Though I don't believe she's the one who witnessed this alleged theft."

"Fair enough," my grandmother said, gently pushing me aside and moving Liza into place.

"If I recall correctly," Ms. Bland went on, "neither of the girls can describe the book at issue. Nor did they see the gentleman leave the room with any kind of document, or a case in which to conceal it."

"That's why I've brought them back today, Ms. Bland," my grandmother said. "We'd like to look at the sign-in log from Tuesday. The young ladies would like to see if they can figure out who might have done the deed."

"But, Mrs. Atwell," the librarian protested, "I can't do that."

"Why not? Is it some sort of secret document? Is there a privacy element I'm not aware of?" Lulu asked. You didn't want to be on the other side of her cross-examination, I'll tell you that. "As best I can tell, the log-in is merely a business record to keep track of who comes and goes on a given day. Who uses which of our prized volumes. May I see it at once?"

Ms. Bland didn't have an answer for my grandmother. "I think I'd better call the front office to ask what protocol is."

"I can picture it now. The next board of directors meeting will have us wasting time on just this kind of folly. Perhaps a trustee will see it your way and endow a lock and key for the precious log," Lulu said, shaking her head. "I'll make a deal with you, Ms. Bland. How's that?"

"A deal? Well, it all depends what you mean."

"Let's all four of us sit down at one of the tables with your sign-in book. All together, out in the open. Totally collaborative and all that. If it turns out that Devlin and Liza are wrong, then not only will you get a most proper apology, but the girls will devote twenty hours of community service to tutoring young readers in your literacy program."

"Excuse me, Mrs. Atwell," Liza said. "To be fair, you have to know that I won't be in the country long enough to commit the necessary hours to keep your promise."

"Then Devlin will have to do forty hours. Simple as that," Lulu said. "Am I right, Devlin?"

"Right as rain, Lu," I said, trying to sound like I meant it. I couldn't figure out what was ever right about rain, but it was one of my grandmother's stock expressions.

"It seems as though I have no alternative but to accept the generous terms of your offer, Mrs. Atwell. Make yourselves comfortable," Ms. Bland said, "and I'll join you with the log."

The librarian was muttering something under her breath.

"She'd better think twice before using language like that in my presence," my grandmother said.

"But she didn't say anything, Mrs. Atwell," Liza said, trying to strike a just balance between these two very uneven teams.

"You just didn't hear her, young lady."

"Atwell ears," I said to Liza. "Best genetic trait I got from Lulu's side."

"What?"

"She can hear like she's got an amplifier in her eardrum. Always could. And her father before her. My mother jokes that she thought it was a super-trait meant for Lulu to spy on her when she was dating my dad."

"You've got it, too?"

"In development, Liza. Working on it," I said. "My grandmother can sit in a crowded restaurant and be chatting us up about her latest cultural outing, and a minute later, she'll tell me that the gentleman at a table across the room just said that the veal chop was the best dish on the menu."

"Have you ever used your Atwell ears on a case?"

"They came in very handy when that five-year-old neighbor of mine let his gerbil out of the cage and the little guy escaped."

"How so?"

"After we scoured the whole apartment, I just sat by myself in the middle of the living room. Nobody around me. Totally concentrating," I said. "About an hour later, I heard this really faint sound, like a scratching of nails on the wooden floor."

"You found the gerbil?"

"Yeah. He'd nested in a pair of slippers in the bottom of the mother's closet. He was running across the floor to get back into the cozy shoe," I said. "Atwell ears broke the case."

"Very cool, Dev."

We settled ourselves at the table closest to the librarians' desk to wait for Ms. Bland to return. Lulu followed us over and sat across from me.

"I've opened the door for you, girls. You're now on your own to prove your case. That's as far as I'm going to take you. A mentor should only put you on the right path, and then let you spread your own wings if you are to be successful at any endeavor."

"That's all we needed, Lu. We're so grateful to you for that."

Ms. Bland returned two minutes later. She sat in the chair beside my grandmother and opened the book to Tuesday's date. "I hope this is helpful to you."

Lulu took the book and turned it around to face Liza and me. Both of us leaned forward in our chairs to see the names. I ran my finger along the list, starting at the top of the page.

My finger stopped on the name of the man who had listed his occupation as rare book and map salesman. He had been at the top of Liza's list of names.

"The man who just left here, Ms. Bland," I said, barely able to contain my enthusiasm. "The man who spoke with the Southern accent. Is he this guy? Is he the map dealer from Atlanta who was in this very room on Tuesday?"

Ms. Bland wiped the lenses of her eyeglasses and took the book back from us. "Yes, yes that's his name. Walter Blodgett. Blodgett Books is his business."

"What volumes was he looking at?" Liza asked.

She stammered. "I—I'll have to check the call slips. I don't quite remember."

"Were you hovering over him like you did with us?" I asked.

"Walter Blodgett is well known to this institution, girls. He *brings* us maps and rare volumes. He doesn't take them. Walter knows some of the acquisitions we'd most like to make and introduces me to people who own them."

"That's how we get many of the valuable treasures that our collection is lacking," my grandmother said. Ms. Bland, grateful for a small show of support from Lulu, pursed her lips and nodded her head so sharply I thought her neck might snap. "A knowledgeable dealer brings us a collector who might have stumbled upon a most unusual find, and would prefer to cash it in or let the world have a look at it. That's the way our collection continues to grow."

"Don't you have everything you need here after one hundred years?" I asked. "The New York Public Library still buys maps and books from people?"

"Well, of course we do, Devlin. Not all the trustees' nickels and dimes go to rebuilding marble pediments or digitizing old books. We're constantly expanding, growing our special collections."

"So what's in it for Walter Blodgett?" I asked.

"Nothing's 'in it' for him," Ms. Bland said. "He's a

great friend of the library. Whenever he comes to New York, he makes time to visit us. Sometimes, Miss Quick, when we get a more valuable map than the copy we currently own, we deaccession ours. We sell it to someone like Walter. It's a very fluid relationship."

"No special privileges for him?" I asked, wondering whether he was a more likely accomplice for a map thief than Jack Williams.

Lulu liked the direction of my questions. I could tell from the trace of a smile that appeared on her lips.

"Privileges?" Ms. Bland asked. "He's very welcome to explore our books and maps. Just as you are."

I lowered myself back into the chair. I knew there had to be a difference between our access to papers of such enormous value and that granted to a trusted friend, but I couldn't put my finger on it yet.

"How about this student?" Liza asked. "This one."

She pointed at the name John Williams.

Ms. Bland looked at the signature, reading his information out loud. "Columbia University. Graduate department of Journalism. This one's a stranger to me."

"Are you sure?" Liza asked. She sounded almost disappointed.

"His name means nothing to me."

"And this one," I said, pointing to the three initials. "You didn't even make him sign his full name."

She leaned in again and looked at the sign-in. "PJS," she said, and gave out with a hearty laugh. "BookBeast. What a silly name for an e-mail."

"Is that what you're laughing about?" I asked.

"That, and because I'm relieved actually, Ms. Quick."

"Relieved about what?"

"You're searching for an evildoer while at the bottom of your list is another friend," Ms. Bland said. "Why, your grandmother knows him practically as well as I do."

Lulu's back stiffened, and she swiveled to face that librarian. "Who might that be?" she asked.

"PJS," Ms. Bland answered. "Preston J. Savage, Mrs. Atwell."

My grandmother practically gasped. "Lovely man, Ms. Bland. A great friend of this library, you're quite right."

"Why, I'd leave him alone with the Gutenberg Bible," the librarian added, glaring at me across the wide table.

I, on the other hand, wouldn't trust him as far as a stolen skateboard could carry me.

19

"What makes Mr. Savage a friend of the library?" Liza asked. "I'd like to be one, too."

"Oodles of money," I said, practically growling my answer.

"Nonsense, Devlin," my grandmother said. "That sourpuss is not the least bit becoming to you, either."

"Mr. Savage is not a wealthy man," Ms. Bland says. "He's very intelligent, and he's devoted to the history of mapmaking and charts."

"But what does he do?" I asked.

"He's an academic. A professor, I believe."

"And just where does he profess to profess?"

"Preston Savage," my grandmother said, enunciating each syllable of his name distinctly, "had an affiliation with Yale University, last I knew. For several semesters, he was visiting faculty at Vassar."

"I knew it!" I said, way too loud for a library. The

baby steps we had followed from the first minutes were growing larger. The path from this room in the NYPL across Fifth Avenue down the ramp inside Grand Central Terminal to the train to Poughkeepsie was becoming easier to follow than the Yellow Brick Road.

"What you *think* you know, Devlin, would barely fill the inside of a thimble," my grandmother said. "Listen to what Ms. Bland has to say about Preston before you jump to any conclusions."

I was beginning to feel like a lesser royal in the Holy Roman Empire that we'd studied last semester, watching family allegiances shift as rapidly as the tides. Why had Lulu suddenly gone cold on me?

"But Lu—"

"Listen to her, Devlin."

My grandmother had pushed back her chair, signaling her readiness to move on.

"Mr. Savage spends much of his time doing research for map collectors," Ms. Bland said. "When a prominent alumnus of Yale bought the private library of an old English family, it was Preston who catalogued the collection for him."

I held the ends of the hair that covered my ears in my hands and twirled them while she talked.

"Inside a very old atlas that probably hadn't been opened in years, he found one of the rarest maps in the world, all folded up and stored there for safe-keeping. Many maps and charts don't live that long because—"

"I know," I said. "Most of them didn't survive because they were actually used by ship captains or soldiers in medieval times. They didn't make it home from the voyages and wars."

"What do you think Mr. Savage did?"

My first instinct was to say that I thought he stole the precious thing, but her question suggested a happier ending for both Preston and the map. "Something noble, I'm sure."

"Sour and snide, too, Devlin," my grandmother said. "Double whammy. I'd advise you to lose them both, young lady."

"Yes, ma'am," I said. When my grandmother was right, she was right as rain.

"Preston convinced the man he worked for to show the map to us, here at the library. He knew it would be our best acquisition of the twenty-first century," Ms. Bland said. "Without Preston Savage, the purchase would never have happened. It's our greatest coup, girls."

"So there's nothing in it for Mr. Savage, either?" Liza asked.

"Our friends are well known to us," Ms. Bland said. "On Tuesday, the very date you're speaking of, Mr. Savage had spent the morning lecturing to some of our curators, upstairs in the boardroom. He was sharing his knowledge with our staff, giving freely of his time."

"What about?" I asked.

"A donor gifted us with a 1680 Thornton map of New England and New York. We displayed it for two days in the boardroom, so that our staff could get to see it first, before the public, and to learn of its importance in our collection."

"Grand idea," Lulu said. "Builds morale when the entire library system is going through so many cuts in funding."

"It is we who benefited most from Preston Savage and his willingness to enlighten us," Ms. Bland said. "I was happy to have him browsing among our treasures when he finished his talk."

"Lovely of you," Lulu said.

"Like Mr. Blodgett—the man from Atlanta who left a while ago—Preston Savage is welcome here anytime he'd like to come," Ms. Bland said.

"Here and at Yale and at Vassar," I said. All places that had collections of rare maps and atlases. "He has access to all your rare books."

"He certainly does," Lulu said.

My own grandmother had turned on me.

And the only difference I could figure so far was that Ms. Bland and her colleagues had no need to hover over Mr. Savage the way she had glued herself to me and my friends on Wednesday afternoon.

Lulu stood up and thanked Ms. Bland for her time. There was also a gracious apology wrapped into her farewell. Then she turned back to me. "More research, Devlin? Staying or going?"

"We'll stay a while," I said. "I like it here. Liza and I want to be friends of the library, Lu. We'll try to think of something good we can do to help here. Isn't that right, Liza?"

Liza just nodded her head, seemingly as perplexed as I was.

Before my grandmother could say her good-byes, Booker Dibble came through the door. Lulu lit up like a Christmas tree when she spotted him.

"Booker! It's been ages," my grandmother said, accepting the hug that he bent down to give her. "Since when have you started wearing spectacles, young man? What's gone wrong with your peepers?"

"All good, Grandma Atwell," he said. "Just trying them out on the fine print."

There was no more hiding this operation, this conspiracy of three, from Ms. Bland. Her eyes widened as Booker addressed Lulu as grandmother. She loved the Dibble boys as much as my mother did and encouraged them to consider her family.

"How come you're so dressed up?" Liza asked as Ms. Bland took her log and returned to her desk. Liza was admiring Booker's navy blue blazer and gray slacks.

"Debate club met this afternoon," he said. "I got here as fast as I could, so I didn't change my clothes."

"Well, you might stay and keep these girls in line, Booker," my grandmother said. "How would you like to put me in a taxicab before you get to work?"

"I'll do that, Lulu," I said. "Happy to do it."

"I'd rather be escorted by a handsome young gentleman any day of the week, Devlin," she said, taking Booker's arm.

I knew she just wanted the opportunity to make sure he understood that Liza and I were walking on eggshells.

"Give me a minute, Grandma," Booker said. He lifted her arm so he could remove his blazer and put it on the back of the chair. "It's really humid outside."

Then he gave Lulu his Dibble-dazzle of a smile and they walked off together, out through the heavy doors of the Map Division.

"I think I've got it, Liza," I said, snapping my finger.

"Got what?"

"The clue that was staring me right in the face this whole time. Lulu's right. All she could do for us is open the door, and now we've got to take it the rest of the way," I said. "Don't you remember what she asked me before we sat down to eat lunch?"

Liza screwed up her face to try to think.

"She wanted to know what secret I was hiding from her, what we were there at her apartment to tell her."

"Yes, I remember that."

I grabbed Booker's jacket from the back of the chair, held it up in front of me, then folded it over my arm, and headed to the exit. "The question Lulu asked was what I had up my sleeve, Liza."

"So?"

"Of course the map thief had a way to smuggle his

20

"Over here, Booker," I whispered when I saw him walking down the long corridor to us. "Don't go back in the map room."

"What are you doing with my jacket?" he asked. "What's going on?"

"Look, we've had our suspect and seen his opportunity, and we learned that his motive is either financial or the sheer selfishness of possessing something rare and beautiful," I said. "But up until this minute, I didn't think we identified his ability to carry out the theft from the library, and that's why nobody believed that Liza saw him steal something."

"And now you know more?" he asked.

"You bet," I said. "Where could you conceal a big piece of paper?"

"You mean right now?"

"Yes."

Booker held up an imaginary sheet of paper and started to fold it in quarters. "I'd downsize it and stuff it into one of my pockets."

"No, no! Suppose it's really old and only worth something if it isn't folded up like an origami bird."

He put his hands on his hips and cocked his head to think.

"Pretend that it's the size of that poster on the wall," Liza said.

"Right," I said. I had one arm in Booker's jacket and ran across the wide corridor. "This says the lecture was last weekend. They won't need that announcement."

I reached up with one hand, letting the arm of the blazer sweep the floor. The moment to sign up to attend WOMEN IN CRIME FICTION: NANCY DREW TO JANE MARPLE had passed. I pulled the colorful poster board from the tape that held it in place, certain that the turnout for the session had been impressive.

The poster was about the size of a large folio page, the size of a medieval atlas.

"Here, you put your jacket on. You're closer to the height of the tall man than I am," I said, tossing it over to Booker.

Then I kneeled on the floor and carefully rolled the poster, from the bottom toward the top, into a small round cylinder, no more than an inch in diameter. I stood up and firmly handed it to Booker, like it was a copy of the Magna Carta.

"Now what?" he asked, fidgeting with the buttons of his jacket.

"Well, now, where would you hide something you wanted to get out of this library, without being stopped by Ms. Bland?"

Booker grinned at me. "Right up my sleeve."

Liza clapped her hands together, and I prompted my friend to give it a try. "Do it, Booker. See if it fits."

He pinched one corner of the poster with his right hand, keeping his left arm as stiff as a board. Like a magician, he guided the cylindrical tube into his sleeve. It went up his arm as smoothly as my grandmother's fur coat slipped over one of her silk dresses.

It didn't look like Booker could bend his arm, but he held both hands out in front of him. "Now you see it, now you don't."

"Let's go," I said. "We've got everything we need from this place."

"You'd better put the poster back on the wall," Liza said.

I rolled my eyes. "Really? Do you think Nancy Drew let every little thing scare the daylights out of her? If

I'd known about last weekend's lecture, I would have insisted you attend. Learn from the ladies who are masters of caper-solving. Backbone, Liza de Lucena. Stiffen up."

I started marching toward the lobby of the library. We weren't stealing a poster. We were tidying up the place, the way I saw things.

Booker waited for Liza to fall in line behind me and he brought up the rear.

There were always two security guards at the front door. One sat next to the entrance, inside the lobby, checking bags of incoming visitors. The other was perched on a stool near the exit door, stopping people on their way out.

I started to lift my book bag onto the table next to the guard, but he just waved me on. "Thanks," I said. "Have a good weekend."

"It's only Thursday by my watch," he said. His eyes were half closed, and I thought he might fall asleep midsentence.

I stepped into the revolving door and pushed against the brass bar. Grumpy guy, I thought. Glad he didn't stop me. As the door moved, Liza followed me into the next section, and Booker into the third.

"Hold it!" I heard the guard yell.

I was on the front steps, ready to come to Booker's aid, as he just kept revolving to go back into the library.

"Not you, young man," the sleepy guard said, patting him on the shoulder. "Young lady, take off your backpack and show me what you've got."

Liza practically froze, caught between two arms of the door. Booker pushed again so she moved on through.

Her hands were shaking as she opened her bag to reveal the contents—only her summer study books for classes at the Ditch.

"Calm down," I could hear the guard say as he escorted her through the door. "I just stopped you 'cause you look as jumpy as a cat on a hot tin roof."

Of course even the security guards at the library were literary.

I took Liza's hand and we ran down the broad steps to the street.

"We'll have to grow you a poker face, Liza," Booker said. "You need nerves of steel to be a detective."

"I—I thought the guard was talking to you, Booker," she said. "That worried me."

Booker stood in the bright sunlight on Fifth Avenue and straightened his arms against his sides.

"Watch this," he said. "Abracadabra."

With his right hand, he reached inside the lip of his left sleeve and slowly pulled the poster board out. It was still curled tight and appeared to be unwrinkled.

He let the thick paper unroll. It was in perfect condition.

"What a great souvenir," I said. "I'd like to hang that in my bedroom, for career inspiration from Nancy and Miss Marple."

"Your mother's the real deal, Dev," Booker said. "What more do you need?"

"She doesn't want me to follow in her footsteps, I don't think. Or else she wouldn't try to stifle my talent for detecting."

"Good point," Booker said.

"Besides," I said, "we've got our suspect, a motive, and now his *modus operandi*. How's that for Latin, Liza?"

"Preston Savage," she said in her quiet voice. "Now we know how he operates."

21

My mother, Sam, Liza, and I had dinner at Serendipity. It had been my favorite go-to place as far back as I could remember, kid-friendly and mega-sized portions. Everybody there had to play with their food, no matter what your ordered, 'cause there was so much of everything it ended up slopping all over the plate. I wasn't an outcast at Serendiptity.

The cheddar burgers were spectacular, and I knew Liza would like the cinnamon-fudge sundae as much as I did. We didn't get interrogated about Lulu until we were all upstairs in the apartment, since Sam had volunteered to come up so he could walk Asta.

"Is your grandmother okay?" my mother asked. "I really owe her a call."

"She's good. Yeah, she said you do. And she wants to accept your challenge about the Red Sox–Yankees matchup."

"Game on," she said.

"Hey, Sam. You're not too tired to walk my pup, are you? Don't want anyone creeping Asta out, like Jack Williams did to us."

"Even when I'm off duty, Devlin, I'm on the job," Sam said. "Eyes wide open all the time. Every good cop knows that."

"Did you happen to remember, Sam, that Louella Atwell is on the board of trustees of the library?" my mother said, turning around to lean her back against the sink.

I kneeled down to put Asta's leash on, stroke her back, and avoid my mother's line of sight.

"Now that you remind me, Commissioner."

"So I'm guessing that the fact that my one and only daughter paid a visit to her beloved Lulu today might have something to do with the stolen book."

"Stolen page, Mom. We never said it was a book."

"With the stolen page that nobody knows is missing. What's your vote, Sam?"

Liza had seated herself at the kitchen table. Her toes were tapping nervously on the floor, about a foot from my hand. I wanted to grab one of her shoes to make it stand still.

"You got to give it to Devlin," Sam said. "She gets twofers on that one. She lights up her grandmother's afternoon and probably gets some inside info on the big book house at the same time."

"Better than that," I said, getting back up. "Lulu took us to the library."

Confession was supposed to be good for the soul. I wasn't convinced of that fact, in the moment.

"What? Your grandmother knows what's been going on and still took you there?" my mother said, holding her glass of ice water against her forehead.

"We didn't want to go, Mrs. Quick," Liza said. "We told her we didn't want to go."

"Don't tell me she used deadly physical force to get you there?"

"You know the drill, Mom. Can't be rude to Louella Atwell," I said. "What was I supposed to do? Wrestle with my grandmother?"

"And because you think I'm not doing enough to help you with your case, of course, she would jump right in on your side," my mother said, taking a sip of her drink.

"No. Not really. I'd say she's totally allied with you

now on this one. She just wanted to hear things from the librarian's point of view."

There was no need to mention that Lulu had started out in our corner but had gone all Benedict Arnold on me once she heard the suspect was her pal Preston Savage.

"What's she up to tomorrow? Another visit?" my mother asked. "Or are you and I keeping on target for Monday?"

"Lulu's going to the country for the weekend," I said. "She's washed her hands of all this."

"Good try, though, kid," Sam said, tousling my hair and then taking Asta's leash from me. "Using all your resources to get at your perp. I like your style."

"Thanks, Sam. I owe most of it to you."

"Homework, anyone?" my mother asked. "Say good night to Sam."

"All caught up," Liza said. "Friday's going to be a light day."

"I'll get some fresh air with Sam and Asta," my mother said. "Then we three can all hang out in the living room and watch TV."

"I'm good with that," I said. "See you tomorrow, Detective Cody."

I wanted nothing more than to get to my laptop and catch up on the news of the Latitude Society players, but I could use this downtime to think. What could I possibly tell Miss Shorey to get out of tomorrow's field trip to the library?

I made it through two episodes of an old public television show about some fancy family in England after World War I. I couldn't relate to anything in it except the fabulous clothes the women wore and the super-cool vintage cars.

"Night, Mom," I said, kissing her on the cheek. "You look whipped."

"I am, babe. Going to sleep now, too," she said. "Good night, Liza. See you in the morning."

I raced to get into my pajamas, onto my bed, and then online.

There was a text from Katie, who was doing a countdown of the days till we left for Montana—only twenty to go—and a brand-new one from Booker.

What's up your sleeve tonight? he asked. Awesome clue.

It was your blazer that made me think, after Lulu's words.

Can U talk?

Best not. Mom's going to sleep early. If she hears, she'll know I'm out of bounds.

K.

Then I remembered another thing. The man you were researching—the rare book dealer from Atlanta—was at the library today, just before you got there.

No way.

Way. His name is Walter Blodgett.

No wonder he doesn't call back. The answering machine at his store in Atlanta, Buckhead Books, says he's traveling and won't be back until next week.

Well, like Mr. Savage, he's a buddy of the library. I'm trying to see if the two are connected or working together. Got to find out what my Latitudians are doing tonight, Booker. Talk tomorrow.

I grabbed my laptop and logged in to the society site. I tried to skim the posts as quickly as I could.

Liza came out of the bathroom and got under the covers. "Anything happening?"

"Interest seems to be building in Saturday's event

in Brooklyn," I said. "And you, my friend, are like a lightning rod."

"I am?"

"Yep. Seems like those comments of yours have attracted a lot of attention—some good, some bad. People are really looking forward to meeting you."

"I think I'm going to try to be incognito, Dev. Is that okay?"

"Whatever."

"Any word from Preston Savage?"

"Total silence," I said.

"You're checking for BookBeast, too?"

"Of course."

"Savage. Beast. Not the most clever way to disguise himself."

"Do you mind if I turn out my light, Dev?"

"Suit yourself, Liza. I'm too wired to go to sleep right now."

I stayed up for another hour, lobbing some controversial posts into the conversation about the Cortés exhibition. I thought it was too risky to say anything more about wanting to meet a book thief. Maybe that was why my contacts slowed down.

* ❋ *

My mother was about to leave the apartment the next morning when Liza and I came into the kitchen for breakfast. Natasha was setting out our cereal bowls and toast.

"Good morning, girls. Sleep well?"

"Yes, ma'am," Liza said.

"That's good," my mother said. "Me too."

"Busy day, Mom?" I asked.

"I'm hoping for a quiet one. You okay walking yourselves to school?"

"No problem. Looks like another nice day."

"Let's stay in touch. The mayor might insist I have dinner with him tonight," she said. "Fourth of July weekend is right around the corner, and we've got to tighten up all the planning for the tall ships in the river and the fireworks display."

"I'll be here, Blaine," Natasha said. "Okay if we order in pizza?"

"It hasn't been the healthiest week of dining for poor Liza."

"Don't worry about me, Ms. Quick. I love pizza."

"Thanks for letting me off the hook," she said. "You've had an action-packed week. I'm glad for the weekend ahead."

We ate our breakfast, walked to school, and went

to our first morning class. Liza seemed more sub-dued than usual.

By the time I was on my way to Miss Shorey's room—with the unsigned permission slip in my pocket—I was still struggling to think of a way out of the field trip.

I stood in a corner of the stairwell and called my mother's office. It wasn't Tapp who answered the phone. "Commissioner Quick's office."

"Hi," I said. "It's Devlin Quick. Is my mother there?"

"No, I'm afraid she's not."

"How about Tapp?"

"Sergeant Tapply's out today with a stomach flu. I'm just answering the phones for him. How can I help you, Dev?"

I was wondering the same thing myself.

"Could you please ask my mom to give me a call when she gets back to her desk? It's nothing urgent," I said. "I just need to ask her about some plans for this afternoon?"

"Then maybe you ought to try her cell, Dev."

"I'm not supposed to bother her when she's work-ing, unless it's something really important. That why I called the office."

"I get it," the officer said. "But she's not likely to be back here until the end of the day."

"Something wrong?" I asked. So much for her quiet day. "Where did she go?"

"She's just fine, Dev. But a patrol car flipped over chasing some perps out in Queens. Sam took her to the hospital so she could be there when the cop comes out of surgery."

"She's the best," I said. She had every good instinct a person should have.

"You got that right."

"Thanks, Officer. I'll talk to her later."

I ended the call and walked to the sunny room at the end of the hallway. Miss Shorey and the other girls in the class were milling around, getting ready to leave.

"There you are, Dev," Miss Shorey said. "Have you got your permission slip?"

"That's just it, Miss Shorey. I didn't mean to hold you all up, but I'm afraid I can't go with you today."

"But, Dev," she said, "it was my conversation with you that gave me the idea to take everyone to the library."

"I know that," I said, handing her the unsigned slip

of paper. "We've got this wonderful girl from Argentina who's staying with us for the first half of the summer session. My mom's assistant promised to give her a tour of One Police Plaza, and this seems like the best afternoon to do it."

"I certainly can't argue with the police commissioner," Miss Shorey said with a smile. "I'm sure the rest of the girls would rather go with you than come with me."

"Not very likely," I said.

We all walked out together, and I spotted Liza waiting for me in front of my locker.

"How did you get out of it?" she asked. "No fiblets, I hope."

"Truth," I said. "Remember on Tuesday when you met Tapp in my mother's office? Remember that he offered you a tour of headquarters?"

"Sure I do."

"I told Miss Shorey about Tapp's promise, and that today seemed the perfect day to go there."

"That's so cool, Dev," Liza said. "And Tapp agreed?"

"He happens to have taken a sick day," I said. "But the fact is it's true that he offered you a tour. Anyone in my mom's office can help with that."

Liza was trying to make herself feel better about the situation. "At least your mom will be glad to have us there."

There was no need to update Liza on the commissioner's whereabouts before we got to One PP.

"Think of it, Liza," I said as we left the school to walk to the subway station on East Eighty-Six Street. "They have the latest computer systems that can do record checks and get any kind of background information you can imagine. This could be our luckiest break yet."

"Devlin Quick," Liza said, sounding more like a big sister than a friend. "What do you think your mother will have to say about this?"

"Didn't you hear Sam last night, Liza? He encouraged me to use all my resources," I said. "My mother didn't object to that, did she? And what could be better than this? There are always clues to be found in the Puzzle Palace."

22

I sent my mother an e-mail when we emerged from the subway and stopped for a hot dog at one of the food trucks in front of headquarters.

"Miss Shorey wanted to take us on a field trip to the library, but I didn't think you'd like that much. Called your office to see if Tapp could give Liza the tour he promised. Heard about the bad accident and Tapp's flu. Thought it would be fun to hang out at your desk."

By the time we cleared security and made our way to the fourteenth floor, my mother had responded. "Sometimes you really do know how to make me happy! It's a good, safe place for you to be. Let Liza be the honorary PC for the afternoon. Love you."

I showed the e-mail to Liza and she laughed.

When we reached the commissioner's office, I introduced both of us to the detective sitting at

Tapp's desk for the day. His name was Richie Marcus.

"So," he said, ushering us into the big office, "I understand from Dev's mother that you're in charge, Liza. She called to ask me to arrange a tour."

"That would be wonderful," she said.

"I'll just get someone to cover the phones here, and I'll take you myself," Richie said.

"We don't mean to put you to any trouble," I said.

"My pleasure, Dev."

"Here's the deal," I said to Liza after he walked out the door. "Eyes and ears on high alert. Let's see if we can do a criminal background check on Savage. There's all kinds of new technology that the department experiments with here, so be on the lookout for anything you think could be helpful, okay?"

"Yes."

Liza had turned her chair around to look out the window. The view across the Brooklyn Bridge, out over the harbor, and then back up the East River was one of the best in the city. Unlike Liza, my mother was all action—or she'd never get anything done from this desk. I had the feeling that Liza would rather stay up here and daydream than keep the city safe.

"That's Brooklyn," I said to her, pointing across the river. "That's where we're going tomorrow."

"It's enormous."

"No kidding. It used to be its own city," I said. "It had nothing to do with Manhattan at all. Till 1898, when they joined up to become the City of New York."

"They're expecting us in the Major Case Squad," Richie Marcus said from the doorway. "Ready to roll, girls?"

"Roger that," I said.

"You've been spending way too much time with Sam Cody," Richie said, patting me on the shoulder as we walked to the elevator.

The Major Case Squad office on the sixth floor of headquarters looked like a movie set for a high-class cop drama. Every desk had hi-tech computer equipment, the walls were lined with file cabinets topped by WANTED posters, and the detectives—all in shirtsleeves with holsters exposed—appeared to be totally engaged in their work.

Richie Marcus walked us to the desk of an African American woman who looked about my mom's age. She'd been expecting us. She was wearing a gray pinstriped suit, and I assumed the bulge on her waist was a gun. Her hair was short and curly, her posture was perfect, and I didn't take personally the fact that she was all business.

Several of the guys gathered around as she explained the work of Major Case. I knew from my mother's conversations with Sam that it was a really elite squad, which is why it was located in One PP and not in one of the precinct buildings scattered around the city.

"... and we handle all the high-profile kidnappings, at the discretion of the commissioner," she said, continuing to list their duties. "We get to partner with the Feds on bank robberies, and we're responsible for art thefts, too."

"Art? Like from burglaries in people's homes?" I asked.

"Not your apartment, Dev," she answered. "I've been there with your mom. But from what I hear, your grandmother might fit the bill."

I blushed.

"Sorry, kid. I didn't mean to embarrass you. More likely we'd get the cases from museums," the detective said. "We investigate burglaries and thefts when the value of the stolen property is over one hundred thousand dollars."

Liza's eyes opened wider at that one. "Did you ever have a case in the New York Public Library?"

"That would mean the disappearance of a whole lot

of books to meet our criteria. Like everything Shake-speare ever wrote," one of the guys said. "Never been there."

Can't help it if these particular cops didn't know the value of the library treasures. This wasn't the moment for me to educate them.

I thanked them as we left the squad.

"At least we know," Liza said, "that if something worth a whole lot is at stake in our case, your mother can assign it to that lady. She looks really tough."

It took the better part of an hour for Richie to take us through the incredibly sophisticated counter-terrorism offices. My mother had devoted a lot of time and money to making it the spiffiest squad of its kind in the country—the most up-to-date and powerful—and she would be proud and pleased that Liza and I spent time there.

The men in TARU—the Technical Assistance Response Unit—did all the work like eavesdropping and wiretaps. They could conceal a tiny camera in the button of a man's shirt to record drug sales, and plant microphones the size of a baby flea in the apartment of a bad guy. I loved to listen in while my mother played back tapes at our dining room table late at night, to hear how heists and hits were planned—and then thwarted by her great detectives.

"We're almost there, Liza," I said as Richie Marcus led us out of the elevator on the eighth floor. "Had to do the full-on tour so my mother knows we were serious, but the next stop is our target."

Liza just nodded. I think all the blue uniforms were making her dizzy.

"So this is one of the jewels in our crown," Richie said. "It's the Real Time Crime Center. It's where I usually work, so I can show you around."

The large room was like the beating heart of the Puzzle Palace.

There were no windows to distract the detectives from their assignments, in which they served as lifelines to cops on the street. On every wall were huge screens that flashed real-time images of police activity, crime scenes, thugs on the lam, and all the up-to-the-second information that would solve cases within minutes of their commission.

The computers on each desktop were the fastest made, and were loaded with everything from criminal records to locations of every registered gun owner in the city to apartments in which police had responded to domestic assaults. It was a giant search engine and a data warehouse to help police officers on patrol the moment they asked for assistance.

Liza was amazed and trying to take it all in. The members of the team on duty were each so busy that most of them didn't even turn their heads away from their screens. A few called out my name and waved, but most were absorbed in their work.

"We're the air traffic controllers of street crime," Richie said to her. "It used to take weeks to get this kind of data to cops in the field, Liza. Mug shots or information about arrest warrants. Everything had to be done by a hand search of records. Now we can do it within minutes."

"Would you please show Liza what you can do?" I asked.

Richie pointed to his desk across the room, below one of the giant screens. "Sure," he said. "Follow me."

Liza and I pulled up chairs on either side of him.

"Here's one from yesterday," he said. "A man walked into a pizza shop on the Upper West Side at four o'clock. Orders a slice to go. The clerk turns his back to cook the slice and when he serves it up, the man has a gun in his hand. Demands all the money in the register. Flees the scene with a pepperoni slice and ninety-six dollars."

Liza gasped and covered her mouth with her hand. "Was he hurt?"

"The clerk? No, he's fine. Describes the gunman—approximate age, height, and weight," Richie said, typing into his computer. The second he hit enter the location of the robbery and the description of the perp appeared on the large screen over our heads. "Still looking for a needle in a haystack, right?"

Liza and I agreed with him.

"There are more than ten million mug shots of men in this system, thousands of them who are white males, about forty, five foot ten inches, and a hundred and fifty pounds."

"Sounds hopeless," Liza said.

"Then the clerk, who's still shaking like a leaf because it's less than ten minutes after the robber left the scene, tells the cop taking the report that the gunman had a tattoo on the hand holding the gun."

"A tattoo of what?" I asked.

"A snake, Dev. A coiled cobra with its head all fanned out."

We watched Richie type the word "cobra" on his keyboard and hit enter again.

"Wow!" Liza said. "That's incredible."

On the screen, there was the mug shot of a middle-aged man with a name and address to go along with the photograph. He lived about four blocks from the pizza shop he had robbed, and he was in the NYPD's tattoo database from the last time he was arrested for mugging a man on Broadway in broad daylight.

"The cops had the perp in custody within the hour, and the clerk identified him in a lineup," Richie said. "Case closed."

Richie held out his hand with a thumbs-up to Liza.

"Show us what else you can do," I said. "It's not just New York City data, is it?"

"I don't have much in here from Argentina, but let's do some test runs," he said. "We can access 911 calls going back a decade or more, those millions of mug shots are from departments all over the country, and there are at least thirty million criminal complaints in the system, so we can compare MOs— that means . . ."

"*Modus operandi*," Liza said. "Got that."

"Yeah, we can even compare them from case to case, with no arrests ever made."

"So take a name like Walter Blodgett, Richie. What happens when you run him through the system?" I asked.

"Is he an imaginary friend, Dev," Richie asked, typing in the name, "or can I really show you two the bells and whistles in my database?"

"He's the real deal."

"I'm trusting that you don't know any criminals, Dev. I can only let you see stuff that's public record."

"He's a businessman, detective. A friend of a friend of mine," I said, referring to my new bestie, Ms. Bland. "It's just more fun to enter a real name than to make one up. That's how my mother always shows my friends."

"That's okay, then," he said. "Looks like we got sixty-seven Walter Blodgetts in the United States. Can we narrow him down?"

"I can help," Liza said. "He's probably fifty years old or more. And he lives in Atlanta."

"Now you're talking," Richie said.

Another keystroke and *our* Walter Blodgett was the only one from the long list that appeared on the screen. His name and home address, business, phone, car, and license plate number—it seemed as though all his major statistics were laid out in front of us.

"Can an ordinary citizen get this info?" I asked, leaning in to skim the words.

"A lot of this information is available online, if you

have the time to search dozens of different sites, Dev. But if you stick with me and my Real Time Crime database, mostly all of it will come up in one place," Richie said. "So you said you actually know this Mr. Blodgett?"

"He's sort of a business associate of our friend," Liza said.

Her confidence level peaked when she was within the safe confines of the palace. I liked her attitude.

"Do you think he ever committed a crime, Liza?" I asked.

She shook her head and almost snickered when she answered me. "Not our Mr. Blodgett. How could you even think that, Dev? He's a friend of—well, he's a friend of Ms. Bland."

Richie was showing off. He cleared the monitor and typed in Blodgett's date of birth along with his name and social security number.

"That's a mug shot!" Liza squealed, pointing up at the screen.

"Isn't it always those guys you don't expect?" Richie asked.

"What did he do?" I almost bounced out of my chair. "Who'd he kill?"

I stood behind Richie, quickly held up my phone,

and took a photo of Blodgett's face without using a flash—not that a mug shot ever flattered its subject. I was certain Richie Marcus didn't see me do it or he might have protested.

Richie laughed. "Nothing that bad, Dev."

"What, then? A theft, right?"

"One collar."

"That's cop slang for an arrest," I said to Liza.

"Collared for assault," Richie said. "Punched a guy in the face."

He was scrolling through the information on the report.

"Who'd he hit, Richie?" I asked. "Where did it happen?"

"The 'who' is a problem. Looks like the vic refused to press charges," he said. "Happened in Massachusetts about two years ago. The case was dismissed because the guy who was hit wouldn't prosecute, so his name's been been taken out of the official documents."

"No fair," I said, backing down into my seat. "Where in Massachusetts? My grandmother would love it if the assault had been at Fenway Park and Mr. Blodgett clocked a Yankee fan."

"Cambridge, Massachusetts."

I slapped my hand on his desk. "That's where Harvard University is, Liza."

"What was the address on the complaint."

"It just says Harvard Yard."

"Does Harvard have a rare map collection?" Liza asked.

"It must," I said, not wanting to derail Richie who was getting such great information for us so quickly. "Can your system do that kind of search?"

"Hey, Dev, my machine can beat the smartest *Jeopardy!* champion," Richie said. "Here goes. Yep, the Pusey Library in Harvard Yard."

"So Mr. Blodgett got in a fistfight outside a rare map collection, Dev," Liza said. "I hope he's on our side of things and not against us."

"Can you run another name for us, Richie?" I asked.

There were dozens of knots in my brain, and I was trying to untangle them and keep all the strings in place.

"Savage," I said, revealing the real purpose of my visit. "What can—?"

"Did you say Savage, as in beast?" he asked.

Liza's mouth dropped open. She was thinking of BookBeast and his xmail address.

"Exactly. Preston J. Savage."

"Are you sure your mother will be okay with this?" Richie Marcus asked.

"She was actually going to have Tapp run this for us on Monday."

"Really?"

"No joke. I mean it's not like we're going public with this. You can ask her on Monday."

"Let's get on with it, then."

Lulu had unlocked the library door that gave us the name of the man Liza saw defacing a rare book. The Real Time Crime Center was bringing him closer to home.

My skin tingled when I saw the information pop up on the screen in black and white.

"Preston James Savage," Richie read aloud. "Male, white. Thirty-eight years old. Single. No children."

"Why isn't there a photograph?" I asked.

"Be patient, Dev. This is just his vital stats."

"Where does he live?"

"LKA was . . ."

"Sorry, but what does that mean?" Liza asked.

"Last known address," Richie said, "was in Garrison, New York."

"Not far from Poughkeepsie, Liza," I said. "Same train line."

"But why is it the last known one?" she asked.

"Could be a lot of reasons," Richie said. "Maybe he moved out, maybe he stopped paying rent, maybe it was just temporary. But he's not getting any mail or bills there now."

"Who's he working for?" I asked.

"Shows him as unemployed. Lists his occupation as teacher, but he's currently not working."

I was trying to keep up with Richie as he read through all the data. "Looks like he had a car. A Honda Civic," he said. "But he sold it last year. There's nothing registered to him now."

"Let's try for a criminal record check," I said, impatient that the body of information about Savage was so vague.

"What's all this about, girls?" Richie asked. "Another business associate or a family friend?"

I grinned at him sheepishly and tried to flash my most innocent look. "What else would it be, Richie? You think we're on the scent of a career criminal?"

"You must have a lot of your mom's DNA, Dev.

That's what I think you're up to. Auditioning to be top cop."

Preston Savage's name and date of birth flashed up on the screen. Below them were the words NO CRIMINAL RECORD.

"No rap sheet, so no photo of Savage comes up. Haven't I worn you two out yet?" he asked, pushing away from his desk. "Why don't we go back upstairs? How about I get somebody to fingerprint both of you?"

"There must be five sets of my prints on file here, Richie. It's how my mom used to keep me quiet whenever she brought me here," I said. "I've got one more thing I think we should show Liza."

"What would that be?"

"So this Preston Savage fellow? Well, he seems to be a friend of my grandmother's," I said. "And she always looks out for me, so I want to make sure to do the same for her."

"That's kind of sweet, Dev," Richie said.

"He used to own a car, right?" I asked. "Why don't you show Liza how your system can even check to see whether something as minor as a parking ticket can sweep you into Real Time Crime?"

Richie looked at his watch and suppressed a scowl.

"Why don't you have Sergeant Tapply do that on Monday, like your mom said?"

"C'mon, Richie," I said. "My mother told me that the worst serial killer in New York City history was caught because of the parking tickets he'd gotten at the crime scenes, decades ago when it took months to get those records by a hand search."

"Are you serious?" Liza asked. "Parking tickets caught a murderer?"

"Son of Sam," Richie said. "That was his nickname."

The Son of Sam arrest was a great moment in the NYPD's history, long before the invention of computers and hi-tech crime-solving strategies. I let Richie brag on about it to Liza while he sat back down at his desk.

Then he plugged in the info about Preston Savage again, asking for a motor vehicle record search from every state in the country.

"Looks like we got a scofflaw, Dev," Richie said as a list of six tickets loaded on the giant screen. "You tell your granny to have her friend pay his bills."

"Will do," I said. "May I ask one more favor, please? Just don't tell my mom that my grandmother's hanging out with a deadbeat, okay? I don't need them to bicker over something like that."

"How's this? You call me on Monday, after Tapp has done his thing for your mom, and then we'll all be on the same page," Richie said.

Mission accomplished. No need for anyone to tell the commissioner about this aspect of our investigation before tomorrow's visit to the exhibition. Liza and I didn't need to be shot down again before we have a chance to make our case.

I was scouring the list while Richie turned to Liza. "Son of Sam was a scofflaw, too. He was stupid enough to land a parking ticket while he was committing a crime."

Savage had managed to get two tickets in New Haven, Connecticut, which may have overlapped with his teaching time at Yale. There were three he picked up in Poughkeepsie—probably also when he lectured there. They weren't recent, of course, since he no longer had a car.

The last one on the list stopped me cold. Somehow the Puzzle Palace never disappoints. Preston Savage had been ticketed when he parked in Harvard Yard, on the very same night almost two years ago that Walter Blodgett had assaulted a man.

Like I always said, in my line of sleuthing, there was no room for coincidence.

23

"That was your mom on the phone," Natasha said to me while I was washing the dishes. "She's about to leave the hospital and grab a bite to eat with Sam. The injured officer came through the surgery well and is going to be just fine."

"What good news," I said.

"She's glad you and Liza had such a great time at One PP. At least she didn't need to worry about what you were up to."

"We had a really interesting tour, and the guys showed Liza all the bells and whistles," I said. "Are you going out tonight?"

"No, I'm staying home to study. And you'd better turn in early because you've got swim practice tomorrow," Natasha said. "Wait till you see her in the pool, Liza. She's a regular speed demon."

"Liza's not coming with me."

"Why not?"

"She's opted for the cooler dude to hang with," I said. "Booker invited her to his tennis practice."

"Aha!" Natasha said with a laugh. "Well, I'll bet there'll be a long line of Hunter girls shooting daggers at you, Miss Liza. Booker seems to have a fan following wherever he goes."

"I happen to like tennis," Liza said.

"Give me a break and just admit it," I said, tugging on her braid. "You have a crush on Booker."

Liza shook her head to brush me off.

"Want me to meet up with you in the afternoon?" Natasha asked.

"I think we'll be good, thanks. The three of us can hang out and figure something to do. We'll all be together with you for the picnic in the park by evening."

"Okay. I'll be in my room reading if you need anything," she said.

"See you later."

I set out my swim clothes for the morning and called Booker to remind him to pick up Liza before he went to practice.

Then I got in bed and opened my laptop. I logged

in to the Latitude Society site and hit the Archives section.

Several years' worth of the newsletters were online. I punched up some random editions going back over time, frustrated by the fact that there was no membership list.

There was a board of directors that changed on the letterhead every couple of years, but no one familiar in that listing. There was a column of items for sale, which seemed to be mostly duplicates of maps of the New England colonies and the coastline of Florida.

And then there was a notice on the back page of just about every newsletter. It was entitled MISS-ING. These weren't the lost children whose faces showed up on milk cartons, but instead hundreds of thousands of dollars' worth of rare maps. And they appeared to be missing from every institution up and down the eastern seaboard.

Rogers's 1816 New Chart of the Gulf of Florida and the Bahama Banks, missing from Harvard; Evans's 1758 General Map of the Middle British Colonies, missing from the New York Public Library; Ellicott's 1792 Plan of the City of Washington, missing from Yale. It looked as though these three great institutions alone were the hunting grounds for at least one greedy thief.

Liza finished her bath and got into bed. "Anything new?"

"Just that we could make a career out of finding rare maps. Stealing them must be a very profitable business," I said. "Who knew?"

"Have you run across any of our names? Walter Blodgett? Preston Savage? Jack Williams?"

"Shhhhh," I said. "Don't let Natasha hear you. She swears Jack's a good guy."

"Maybe he is, but that was still weird the other night."

"Here's something! There was a special exhibition at Harvard, at the Pusey Library, on the very date that Blodgett punched an unidentified man and Savage got a parking ticket."

Liza leaped off her bed in a flash and crowded next to me on the bed.

"What was it?"

"It was an exhibition of Samuel Champlain's 1613 map of New France," I read to Liza from the archived newsletter, "described as the single most important map in Canadian history."

"Did we—I mean the Latitude Society—put on the exhibition?" she asked.

"No, the Harvard Library sponsored the event."

"Any names?"

"No names," I said, every bit as disappointed as Liza was. "Three possible perps—working alone or maybe even in a ring of criminals, and not a single name is here."

"Don't give up, Dev. Let me go through it again."

"Sure," I said, turning my laptop over to her. "You're more careful than I am anyway."

Liza gave the words on the screen her most intense stare. Then she pushed it away and leaned back against the wall.

"It's a dead end, right?" I asked.

"Seems to be."

We were both bummed.

"Wait a minute, Liza," I said, retrieving my laptop and going back into the society's archives. "Some member usually reports on the events after they happen."

"When was the next newsletter?"

"That's what I'm checking for," I said. "Looks like two months after the Champlain exhibition."

I scanned it carefully but there was nothing about the show at the Harvard Library.

"Nothing. Nothing at all."

"Don't give up, Dev. That's not like you," Liza said. "Try the next issue."

I found a newsletter dated four months after the Champlain exhibition. "Fingers crossed. Here's a mention."

My eyes darted across the page, searching for highlights to read. "'Well attended,' 'catered by blah-blah-blah', 'Boston's Mercator Association was represented by Alexandra Denman'—she's an old chum of Lulu's—blah-blah-blah. Here! Liza, it's here! 'The Latitude Society contingent was led by Walter Blodgett.'"

"Good work, Dev."

"Yes, Blodgett was sipping cocktails in the presence of an original Champlain just a few hours before he belted somebody in the nose."

I continued to read, but there were no other names of note.

"Was the Champlain ever stolen?" Liza asked.

"Doesn't appear to be. It's in a private collection somewhere."

Liza went back to her bed and got under the covers. "Has anyone from the Latitude Society contacted you today?"

"I'm about to log in," I said.

I used Liza's screen name and opened my account. The first three e-mails were blasts about tomorrow's event. People who were looking forward to seeing the great Cortés map and so on. The fourth one was meant for me. "Ouch!"

"What happened? Are you all right?"

"Yeah, just some nameless dude telling me not to be so stupid as to talk about wanting to meet a thief," I said. "Look, he can't possibly know I'm just trying to smoke out a bad guy at the exhibition. After all, he's right."

"But what's his e-mail name?"

"Nothing familiar, Liza. It's not one of our guys, unless he's changed his e-mail address. We might find out soon enough."

"Did you reply to him? I mean, did I?"

"Just a blast back to the crowd," I said. "What I wrote was 'Remember the Champlain! Remember Harvard Yard! Let's hope there is no similar revenge of Montezuma!'"

"I get the point that you're trying to start some controversy, Dev. But why do you think Blodgett's punches have anything to do with the library?"

"They've just got to, Liza. The rare map business is so high stakes, as we're finding out more and more every day. The fact that he assaulted someone just outside a once-in-a-lifetime exhibition is most likely because tempers flared and there was an argument. We just have to find out what that was about."

"But how?"

"Put it out of your mind for now," I said, powering down my laptop.

"But it makes me nervous, Dev, if you don't even know how we're going to handle this tomorrow."

"I have to sleep on it, Liza. I just don't have an answer for you right at this moment."

And to tell you the truth, that made me nervous, too.

24

My mother came in at the crack of dawn to kiss me good-bye and make sure my alarm was set. At seven thirty, when it rang, Liza and I dressed for the day. I put on a turquoise polo shirt for the exhibition, figuring my jeans and sneakers would be necessary if we developed any good leads.

Booker came by at eight forty-five in a yellow cab to pick up Liza. She was so excited about her outing with him that I was afraid all the adrenaline she'd need to investigate at the Brooklyn Central Library would be used up sitting courtside.

"When and where do we meet up?" he asked.

"Let's say Eighty-Sixth Street and Lexington Avenue at eleven fifteen," I said. "The exhibition opens at noon, and I've mapped out the subway route."

"Cool," Booker said. "Swim fast."

I was so wired that I practically ran to the Ditch. I stopped in front of Miss Wilhelmina to do my curtsy. She had given me such a leg up by instilling in me the We Learn, We Lead motto that I believed in its power even more with the events of this week.

The pool was in the basement of the school. The intense humidity enveloped me as soon as I opened the door and went into the locker room.

"Hey, Dev," one of my teammates said. "Good to see you. Are you doing summer school?"

This was our first practice since the end of the last semester's exam period.

"Yeah. It's been kind of interesting, actually."

I slipped into my racing suit—a kind of nauseating shade of bubble-gum pink, since pink and gray were the Ditchley colors.

"I am, like, so glad my mother didn't make me do it," Kelly said. "I'm just getting to hang out and have fun for a change. No school, no books. It's like I don't do anything at all every day."

Kelly did a mean backstroke, but she didn't seem to care about her schoolwork. I didn't think I could live without books. "Sounds good, Kelly."

There were at least a dozen girls warming up in the pool by the time I got to the end of one of the lanes.

"Jump in and get going," the coach said to me, waving her arm. "Glad you're here, Dev."

The water was a brisk seventy-eight degrees, and it actually felt good to be in it. I did about ten laps before the coach blew her whistle and called us all out to the end of the pool.

We spent the first half hour exercising, which was a routine I had let slip during this investigation. We weren't allowed to do serious weights yet, because of our ages, but we did all our standing moves with five-pounders.

I hated push-ups, which came next—fifty of them today—but they were also essential to building the upper-arm strength so necessary to swimmers.

"Let's try a few heats, ladies," the coach said. "Breaststroke first for a change. I'll mix the order up today."

I sat with my knees drawn up against me, my arms wrapped around my legs, and my chin resting on top. All I could think about was stolen maps, which was not what I needed to focus on right now.

Kelly dominated the next round of swimmers with her backstroke. She realized she was a cool girl and she carried herself like a champion. I'd never know how to do that.

"Four of you for freestyle," the coach boomed in her loudest voice. "Stop dreaming, Dev. Lane one for you."

Next to the green chair in Miss Shorey's library, the pool was the happiest spot in school for me. I was part of a team, but once I had my face in the water and set my own pace, I took off like a jet plane and was totally in a zone of my own.

"Get in your places, ladies," the coach said. "I want to see you explode out of the starting blocks, okay?"

I stepped up and positioned my feet, the left on the edge of the block and the right one behind me.

"Stand tall, ladies," she said. "You, too, Dev. You're a skinny twig now, aren't you? It's all going into your height."

I leaned over, my hands touching the front of the block. The coach barked out the words. "On your marks, get set—GO!"

I dove in, stretching my arms out in front of me and tucking my head in the water. Most of the time at swim meets, my teammates stood on the side of the pool, winding their arms around like windmills, urging one another on by screaming "Faster! Faster! Faster!" and "Stroke! Stroke! Stroke!"

For me, they had come up with a special incentive.

I liked swimming, in part because I couldn't hear the cheering—or jeering—when my head was in the water. I just motored on and did what I was able to do, swimming for my own personal best.

But when I kicked off the wall and came up for air, I could always hear the chant that emphasized my name to motivate me: "*Quick*-er! *Quick*-er! *Quick*-er!" And most days I responded to it.

I was the third swimmer to touch the wall. I threw my head back and ripped off my cap. "Sorry, Coach," I said, after congratulating the girls who beat me.

"What's up, Dev? Have you lost your concentration?" she asked.

"Temporary thing, Coach," I said, trying to catch my breath. "I'll have it back by next week."

"Everything okay? You seem to be somewhere else."

"I'm fine, thanks. I just have a lot on my mind."

I was totally somewhere else—on the number 4 train, trying to remember where I could make the transfer to the 2 or 3.

I went back into the locker room to shower and dress. I checked my phone for messages and e-mails but there were none. I said my good-byes and went out into the sunlight—another hot day—and walked west to the Eighty-Sixth Street station.

Booker and Liza were waiting for me, and we jogged down the long staircases to the subway platform together.

"Did Liza fill you in?" I asked. "Real Time Crime and all that?"

"I'm up to speed, Dev," Booker said. "Have you got a plan?"

"I'm figuring that Walter Blodgett is likely to be there," I said. "He's been in New York all week—we saw him on Thursday afternoon—and his answering machine says he'll be away from his shop till Monday. I can't believe he'd have this opportunity to see something as rare as Cortés's 1524 map without staying on in New York."

"And Preston Savage?" Liza asked.

"He's a bit more of a wild card. No job, no car, no home that we know of. It's just in my gut that he has something to do with this," I said. "And Sam says it's a really basic rule of policing that you go with your gut."

They both nodded in agreement.

"Blodgett's your job for the day, Booker," I said, forwarding to him the photo I took of his mug shot on the giant screen over Richie Marcus's desk. "If we see him, it'll be your assignment to try to chat him up."

"Why's that?" he asked.

"Because you've got that maturity thing going on, like I told you," I said. "He'll take you more seriously than he will either one of us."

"Got it."

"And you can ask him about the night at Harvard," Liza said. "About why he hit a man, and who it was."

"Now, how am I supposed to know that he assaulted someone?" Booker asked. "That charge was dismissed."

"Good point," I said. "Well, we know from the Latitude newsletter that he was there. That's how you can get into the subject."

"How about me?" Liza asked

"Keep an eye out for Natasha's friend Jack Williams," I said. "He's supposed to be studying the famous Manhattan grid. If he shows up here, it might be he's connected to the thief or thieves."

"Poor Natasha," Liza said. "I'd hate for that to be the case."

"We have to go where the evidence leads us, Liza," I said, echoing another Sam Cody mantra.

"What about you, Dev?" Booker asked.

"I'll be looking for the tall man. I'm pretty certain

he's Preston Savage," I said. "We don't have a photograph of him, but I know exactly what he looks like. It was only five days ago that we chased him all the way through Grand Central."

"What will you do if you see him?" Booker asked again.

"Well, if he's really such a scholar as Ms. Bland thinks, and he's really such a friend of the library as Lulu believes, he'll behave like a gentleman. He doesn't have any record of violence," I said. "I just want to talk to him. Confront him with what Liza saw him do, as long as you guys are nearby to back me up."

The subway car pulled into the station, and we got on when the doors opened.

Liza grabbed the pole in the middle of the car and clung to it with both hands like her life depended on it. "What if I'm wrong about what I saw, Dev?"

"This is a fine time to come up with that idea. Backbone, Liza. That's all you need."

"So I've got Blodgett and you've got the tall man," Booker said.

"And if I don't happen to see Jack Williams, which one of you should I be hanging out with?" Liza asked.

"I'll leave that choice up to you," I said. "You can shadow Booker."

I saw a glimmer of a smile on Liza's face.

"Or if you want to face off with the map thief you identified all by yourself, you're welcome to work with me."

Liza de Lucena looked from Booker's face to mine. "I've been in your hands since the first minutes after the crime," she said. "And you're the only person who never questioned what I told you, Dev."

She hesitated before she spoke again. "I'm in this with you all the way. I'd like to be your partner till we make a collar," she said.

"Sounds like you not only picked up some clues in the Puzzle Palace," I said, "but some cop talk as well."

Liza lifted her head up and flashed me a smile. We had really become partners in crime.

25

We transferred to the number 3 train at Nevins Street and reached Brooklyn's Grand Army Plaza shortly before noon.

My phone was ringing as we reached the sidewalk. "Hello?"

"Devlin Quick?"

"Yes. Who's this?"

"I'm one of the librarians at Vassar College. President Hill asked me to call your grandmother with some information about an event we held a few weeks ago. Her housekeeper said Mrs. Atwell was out of town but she would pass me through to you."

I stopped in my tracks. "That's so kind of you."

Booker and Liza flanked me on either side and waited for me while I talked.

"You wanted the list of names of the attendees, am I right?"

"You are."

"If you give me a fax number, I'll send them along."

"It's sort of urgent, ma'am. If you don't mind, we know it's a short list—would you just read them out to me?"

The librarian went through the alums and donors who'd been at the launch party for the Ortelius and Mercator showing. There were only sixteen names, and not one of them was familiar to me.

"How about Walter Blodgett?" I asked.

"I'm afraid I don't know him," she said. "Was he supposed to attend?"

"I—I don't know. My grandmother was hoping he had," I said. "And Preston Savage isn't on your list, either, is he?"

The librarian didn't speak for thirty seconds.

"No . . . but . . . No, he's not."

"What's the 'but' about? Do you know Mr. Savage?"

"I do know him, as a matter of fact. He used to teach here, for a brief period of time," she said. "May I ask, Ms. Quick, how old you are?"

I cleared my throat and tried to deepen the tenor of my voice. "Old enough," I said, "to be assisting my grandmother with her affairs, madam. She's keenly interested in your library, and in the goings-on of Preston Savage."

"Perhaps I should clear this with President Hill before I discuss it with you," the librarian said.

"Discuss what?" I said, imitating Lulu at her sternest. "You should let me be the judge of what's relevant in this matter. My grandmother does."

The librarian didn't resist for very long. "Preston Savage did not attend the Mercator-Ortelius event that evening in early June," she said. "But he was here in the library at the very same time."

"He was? And how do you know that?"

"Because I helped him out, Ms. Quick, while all the others were at the reception."

"What did you do, exactly?" I asked.

"He wanted a carrel, he told me, in which to do some research."

"A carrel? What's that?"

"They're small desks, partitioned off from the rest of the room, or study cubbies in libraries, like college libraries in particular," she answered. "And I guess you're not quite as old as I thought if you've never worked in one."

"Busted," I said to Liza and Booker, covering the

mouthpiece of my phone. "And by a librarian, no less."

"Why did Mr. Savage want a carrel?"

Why didn't he want to be at the important exhibition, and why did he need a private space in which to make his observations?

"There was a book he wanted to see, Ms. Quick. That's my job, you understand."

"According to my grandmother," I said, opting for the softer touch, "Mr. Savage is a great friend of the New York Public Library. He has access to their collection, too, so I get it completely."

Booker nodded to me. "Lure it out of her," he said. "Well done."

"That's why I gave him what he asked for, Ms. Quick."

"Of course," I said. "And do you recall what book that might have been?"

"Certainly," she said. "It was one of our rarest volumes. John Smith's 1625 *Atlas of Virginia*."

"Thank you for your candor, madam. And would you mind a piece of advice from a young person—well, a kid, actually—like me?"

"I'd welcome it."

"I'd suggest you locate that book right now and secure it in a very safe place."

"Why is that?" she asked. "You make it sound quite sinister."

"I don't mean to do that at all," I said. "It's just that the Major Case Squad of the New York Police Department might need to take a look at it next week. The atlas might contain evidence of a crime."

26

"You scored some useful information about Preston Savage," Booker said. "He was at Vassar—at the very time of the party for the Ortelius-Mercator exhibition—but he didn't attend it. I wonder why not."

We were walking across the plaza toward the rear of the Brooklyn Central Library, which resembled the spine of a giant book.

"And he might have been at Harvard for the Champlain display," Booker said, "but didn't go to the opening night reception. What's up with that?"

I was trying to make sense of Preston Savage's actions, to find a pattern in his behavior, if there was one to discover. "We should know soon enough."

We walked around to the front of the building, on Eastern Parkway, and Liza stood still at the base of the library steps, looking up at the impressive structure before us. "It's—well, it is a book, isn't it?"

None of us had ever visited here before. The huge limestone building—at least fifty feet tall—was in fact built in the shape of an open book, and above the entrance there were more than a dozen bronze panels with golden figures in each of them—figures representing beloved characters from American literature.

For a moment, each of us forgot the purpose of our visit, transfixed by the images above our heads.

"There's Hiawatha," Booker said, "and White Fang."

Liza picked out Moby Dick, the Raven, and Rip Van Winkle.

I was whisked back to childhood by the gilded image of Wynken, Blynken, and Nod—fishermen three—sailing off in a wooden shoe. Then I recognized Louisa May Alcott's Meg, who was one of my favorite fictional friends.

"Time for enjoying all this later," I said. "We've got work to do."

People of all ages were pouring in and out of the library as we entered the building. There was an information booth in the center of the lobby, and I approached it to ask about the Latitude Society meeting. We were directed to a room on the second floor.

I suggested to Booker that we enter separately,

so Liza and I approached the conference room first. There was a volunteer at the door—a woman who appeared to be older than my mother—who had a clipboard with a list of names.

"Good afternoon," she said. "Are you members of the society?"

Liza was our mouthpiece. "No, not exactly. But my mother is, and we're supposed to meet her here."

"What's the name?"

"De Lucena. Liza de Lucena."

"I see it here. Plus one."

"That's me."

"So that would make three of you?" the volunteer asked.

"Yes, but—"

"I'm sorry," she said, shaking her head at Liza, "but we've had to limit the numbers because of the response we got to the reception. Two people per ticket. Why don't you wait for your mother—perhaps in the Youth Wing downstairs—and come back when she gets here?"

To me, the woman offered a lame "Sorry, dear."

"But I'm the one doing a paper on *Señor Cortés*," I said. "It's why Mrs. de Lucena invited me. It's so important I get to see the map."

"The exhibit will be open to the public in another week. You can come back then. In the meantime, you'll enjoy the Youth Wing, I'm sure. Fun to browse around. Juvenile fiction and that kind of thing."

Normally, I'd head right for the juvenile fiction section, but I hated being kept out of the exhibition. I steamed a bit as others passed by me and had their names checked off on the list.

Booker started to walk toward us, and I grabbed the sleeve of his shirt. "You'll actually need your glasses this time. This lady has a thing about kids."

Booker reached into his pants pocket and put the reading glasses on his nose as he walked toward the woman. He looked like a full-on scholar. "How are you doing today, ma'am? Booker Dibble here."

"I don't see the name," she said, running a finger down the list.

"I just joined the society the night before last— maybe my online credit card payment didn't catch up yet."

My kind of detective. He had gotten totally into the swing of things and joined the Latitudians in preparation for this visit.

"Here you are," she said. "We had you backward. Dibble Booker."

"It's not the first time someone has made that mistake."

"Go right on in, Mr. Dibble."

I felt queasy for the first time today. I hadn't expected to be separated from Booker quite yet.

"Excuse me, ma'am," I said, approaching the woman again. "I think I just saw a friend of mine go in. Booker Dibble's his name. I can be his guest, can't I?"

But Booker was already out of our line of sight, with people crowding into the room to get close to the Cortés masterpiece.

"He didn't list a guest, dear. Wait for your friend's mother, and we'll see what we can do for you then."

I turned away and took out my phone, scooting down the hallway followed by Liza.

I tried to get a signal but was having trouble. Maybe it was the thick walls in the library and the fact that I was nowhere near a window. I ran across the hallway to see if the reception was better, with no luck.

The security guard was keeping an eye on me. I held the phone up in the air, high over my head, to see if I could make it work. All I seemed to be doing was getting in the way of the flow of visitors.

I stepped off to the side and texted Booker as fast as I could move my fingers. U R out of sight. Come back 2 us.

A security guard walking to the elevator came toward me. "You need to put your cell phone away, young lady. This is a library."

"Yes, sir. I will, but I'm just waiting for a text. I don't intend to talk to anyone."

"This is a really old building, miss. Thick walls and steel foundation. Texts don't usually work inside here anyway. And phone calls certainly don't," he said. "So I'd advise you to put your phone away, like I said."

I took one more glance at the cell screen before putting the phone in the pocket of my jeans.

"Why don't I go in and bring Booker out?" Liza asked. "That lady will let him go back into the exhibit after he talks to you."

"Good idea." I didn't exactly count on being by myself and unable to get through to Booker and Liza, but this was—after all—a public library on a Saturday afternoon. It wasn't exactly a high crime neighborhood.

"Be right back," she said, squeezing my hand. "Why don't you go down to the information desk and wait for us there? That way this lady won't think we're just lurking around."

"Okay, Liza. Good plan."

I took the staircase down and headed for the information desk. I suddenly had an idea that might help us put things together.

When I got to the front of the short line, I asked the woman who was also wearing a button that said VOLUNTEER if she could help me with a problem. She was cheerful and willing to do so.

"I know I can't use my phone here," I said, "so I'm wondering whether you can call one of your other branches from your extension. There's a particular librarian who can answer a question for me."

"Yes, we're all connected in our phone system," she said, picking up the receiver to dial. "If you don't know her number, just tell me what the librarian's name is and where she works."

"It's Ms. Bland," I said. "She's at the main branch on Fifth Avenue."

"Oh," the volunteer said, putting down the receiver. "In Manhattan?"

"Is that a problem?" I asked.

"Not really. It's just that this library is not part of the New York Public Library system," she said.

I was so anxious to talk to Ms. Bland, I couldn't believe the two boroughs weren't connected. "But—but you're part of New York City."

"Yes, but Brooklyn has its own library system—this central building and fifty-eight neighborhood branches—so I'm afraid I have no way of connecting you to the librarian you want to speak to," she said. Then she pointed to the front door. "Why not step outside and use your cell phone if this is so urgent?"

I worried that once I stepped outside, Booker and Liza wouldn't know where to look for me.

I waited another two minutes but there was no sign of my friends. I walked out the front door, down the steps, and off onto the grass to get out of the way of the people on the sidewalk and dialed information to get the number for the New York Public Library.

It took another two minutes to get through the switchboard and transferred to the Map Division.

"Ms. Bland, please?"

"Sorry," the man who answered said. "She's on her lunch break. May I give her a message?"

"Please. Yes, please do," I said, trying to keep calm. "My name is Quick. Devlin Quick."

"Will she know what you're calling about?"

"Not exactly," I said. "But I need her to call me back

and tell me what book Preston Savage was looking at on Tuesday. What kind of maps are his specialty, okay?"

"Let me have your number, please, Ms. Quick. I'll give her that message."

I thanked the man and turned my phone off again, pocketing it to go inside the library.

As I walked through the door, I could see Liza circling the information desk with a sort of panicked expression on her face. She must have been looking for me while I was outside making my call.

"Liza!"

"Dev," she said. "There you are. Didn't you see him?"

"See who?"

"Mr. Blodgett. Walter Blodgett. He must have been getting off the elevator on the second floor just as you got on to come downstairs."

"I didn't take the elevator. That's why I missed him," I said. "Does Booker know?"

"Yes, I pointed him out," Liza said, taking deep breaths between sentences. "Mr. Blodgett just entered the exhibit upstairs."

"Is Booker talking to him?"

"Not yet. Lots of people are greeting Blodgett.

He knows everybody in the society and most of the other guests who've already arrived. From the looks of things, it will probably be fifteen minutes to half an hour before Booker gets him alone to make an approach."

"Fifteen to thirty minutes?" I said. "That's a lifetime. By then it will be almost Monday and this will drop into Sergeant Tapply's lap. Cold Case Squad, here we come."

"Booker's watching Blodgett like a hawk, Dev. That's for sure."

"And no sign of Preston Savage?" I asked.

"Not a trace."

I closed my eyes, cracked my knuckles, and counted to ten. "I have an idea, Liza."

"What kind of idea?"

"The way I figure it, Liza, is that Preston Savage never planned to come to this exhibition today."

"Why not? Forty-eight hours ago you were sure he would show up here. You don't think he's interested in a mapmaker like Cortés?"

"Two different things, Liza. I'll bet you that he's here all right. In this library, but that he won't show his face upstairs, where Booker is."

"Why not?"

"Think of the show at Harvard, the reception in Poughkeepsie, and the lecture he did on Tuesday at the New York Public Library, and now this exhibition about Cortés, who is so controversial," I said.

"Yes, Dev. What's your point?"

I put my hand on my stomach to stop the fluttering butterflies. If Liza knew I was harboring them, she'd run for the nearest exit.

"The well-publicized exhibition," I said, "the big show or the display of the latest rare and valuable thing? It's just a distraction to Savage. That's just the kind of distraction a map thief needs to do his work."

"You mean—?"

"Yes, I mean that everyone important, all the staff and trustees and donors, are completely engaged in the fireworks of the big exhibition. That gives Mr. Savage a perfect opportunity to be alone with the things he loves most in the world—old atlases with scores of valuable pages, ready for the cutting. And the people who give him the books do so because he's cultivated their friendship over time. They trust him completely."

I started walking to the information desk again.

"So you're convinced that he'll show up here

today?" Liza asked, a few steps behind me but trying to keep up with the strides of my longer legs.

"Better than that," I said. "I'm quite sure he's here right now."

"But, Dev," she said, "what makes you think we can find him? We've never been to this library before."

"We've got half an hour while Booker twiddles his thumbs waiting for Walter Blodgett to talk to him," I said. "All I want is five minutes alone with Preston Savage."

27

"What can I do for you now?" the volunteer at the desk asked.

"Carrels," I said. "Where would we find your carrels?"

She looked puzzled.

"You do know what carrels are, don't you?" Although the word was new to me, I assumed a library volunteer would have it down.

"Certainly. I just didn't hear you correctly," she said. "Most of our carrels are on the lower level, in the basement. You can take the elevator or the stairs to your left.

"Thanks so much."

"Want me to run up and get Booker, Dev?"

"Every minute that goes by, Liza, could be another rip through the heart of a book. That's a painful thought, isn't it?"

Whatever focus I had lost during the morning swim practice had come roaring back to me now when I needed it most. I was striding to the staircase while Liza kept her eyes on the elevator doors, as though willing them to open with Booker inside.

"C'mon, partner," I said. "I think I'm right about this."

"What will we do if you are?"

"Easy enough. Either Mr. Savage agrees to talk to me, or if he isn't cooperative, then when I give you the signal, you just turn around and run right back up the stairs," I said. "Go outside and call Sam Cody. You have his number. Or dial 911. There are a whole lot of security guards near the entrance, too."

The stairs were wide and steep, and as we wound down and passed through the second landing, the corridor grew dimmer and darker.

At the bottom of the steps, I came to a stop. Liza was a few feet behind me, but pulled up right by my side. Our sneakers didn't make a sound—not even a squeak—on the old linoleum floor of the basement.

I mouthed two words to Liza. "Follow me."

Slowly I inched forward and was relieved that the lights in the hallway were a bit brighter than those in the stairwell.

There was a long row of carrels on either side of the corridor. As we walked in, it appeared that only two were occupied. There was a kid a bit older than us, who was using library books—it seemed to me—to do homework assignments on her laptop. There was also a man taking notes from a worn volume that had only text—no maps or pictures.

When we reached the end of that row, there was a single line of carrels that was perpendicular to the main one. This part of the hallway was completely dark to the left, but to our right, one carrel seemed to be lighted from a lamp hanging above it.

I made the choice and turned right. I took two steps in that direction and was startled when an overhead light suddenly turned on. Liza clasped her hand on my shoulder, from behind. Being nervous was a contagious condition. I'd been fine till she grabbed me.

I didn't want to speak to her. I didn't want to announce our presence, in case anyone was around who was expecting some level of privacy. It was pretty obvious that the light was activated by a motion sensor, probably an effort to save the library money so it wasn't wasting electricity when the carrels were unoccupied.

I bent over and looked under the row of desks

ahead of me. The well-lit carrel was the very last one to my left. A pair of men's legs was planted on the floor beneath the writing table. The shoes looked, from the back, like the kind the tall man had been wearing the day of the theft.

I straightened up and signaled to Liza—at least I thought I did—to stay here, nearest the long aisle that led back to the stairwell.

I walked in the direction of the seated man, and the next overhead light popped on. I looked back and saw that Liza was following me, which was not exactly what I had planned. Liza and I both stood still.

I took her hand and pulled her into the next carrel with me. There was no way we could get any closer to the man without each light going on and alerting him to our approach.

I had to think.

"What do we do?" she asked, in her softest whisper. "Is it Savage?"

I shrugged my shoulders and shook my head. Then I pointed my index finger to my temple. "Thinking," I mouthed to her.

I knew my phone wouldn't work, but I texted a message to Booker that Liza and I were in the basement, and that I thought we had found Preston Savage. I hit send, figuring even if he didn't get it till after we were all together, he'd know I'd tried to do the right thing.

And then it happened. I heard the sound.

My eyes narrowed, and if I'd been a hunting dog, my ears would have stood straight up. I'd have been a pointer.

Liza heard nothing. That was clear to me.

Again I heard the same sound. Atwell ears at their sharpest, and I thanked my lucky DNA stars to have inherited them from Lulu. I waited before I sprang into action.

The noise stopped for several seconds, and then it started again. It was the sound of paper being torn. The very old fibers of the page of a book were being severed from each other.

I bolted from our carrel and ran fifteen yards toward the man at the end of the row. The lights blasted on overhead, one after another, barely able to keep up with me as I ran.

The man stood up at the sound of my steps and the flood of light. He turned to look in my direction.

It was the tall man, the man we had chased from the steps of the public library.

"Preston Savage," I said, coming to a stop just two feet away from him.

"It's you again," he said. "It's both of you."

He stepped into the aisle, his back against the wall at the very end of the hallway, after he pushed the large atlas he'd been tearing across the desk, farther away from us.

"Mr. Savage," I said, despite the feeling that my heart was trying to push its way into my throat. "We just want to talk to you."

"How do you know my name?" he asked, inching farther to his right.

"We just have a couple of questions to ask you," I said, trying to channel Sam Cody's advice about how to conduct a composed interrogation. "We just—"

Preston Savage had no intention of waiting for me to ask him anything. He spun around, put his hands on the bar that opened the heavy door behind him—under an unlighted red sign that said EXIT—and before I could finish my sentence, he leaned against it and burst through.

28

I pushed against the closing door with my right
shoulder. "Run upstairs, Liza," I said. "Just run.
Grab the kid who's in one of those first carrels working on her laptop and get help."

Liza seemed to be frozen in place. She was fum-
bling with her cell phone.

"It won't work down here, Liza. Now, just go for
backup, will you? Get Booker, too!"

The door was trying to shut against my weight. I
pushed again and shimmied through it, at the top of
more steps that led down into the total darkness of
the sub-basement of the library.

The last sliver of light was behind me.

Suddenly, as I tried to get my iPhone out of my
pocket to use the flashlight on it, the door opened
again. This time it was Liza.

"You've got to get someone to help us, Liza," I said

as the door slammed shut and darkness enveloped us.

"I couldn't leave you alone, Dev. I just couldn't do it."

She was looking to me for courage, I knew, but I was fresh out.

"Friends for life, Liza," I said, although I wasn't sure how long that would be. "Thanks for that."

I reached for her hand and squeezed it with my free one. With the other, I turned on the small beam on the end of the phone.

The steps were painted black and were very steep.

"No point going down there," I said. "Let's get out while we can."

"Yeah," she said.

She pivoted and reached for the handle of the thick old door. She pulled on it but there was no give.

"Let me try," I said. I twisted it and yanked at it several times, but there was no doubt that it had locked behind us.

Again the two of us stood still and again we listened. This time I heard nothing.

"What do you think is at the bottom of the stairs?" she asked me with a serious tremor in her voice.

"The great thing about libraries," I said to her, "is

that the basement levels often go on down forever, and they're filled with stacks, with shelves of books. There are eight levels of stacks of books below the street at the public library in Manhattan."

Books were the only good thoughts, the only safe ones, that I could conjure in this hostile space.

"Then I think you're going to be very disappointed when you get down below," Preston Savage said.

He was so close to me I almost tumbled off the top step at the sound of his voice. He had been hiding off to the side—so still I hadn't heard him breathe—behind a thick beam. Now he stepped into the range of my light.

"March, girls," Savage said. "Go on down."

I thought of the way both my grandmother and Ms. Bland had praised this man. "You don't have to do anything crazy, Mr. Savage. We know you're a friend of all the people at the library."

"How would you know that?" he asked. "To whom have you talked about me?"

Not my first mistake—acknowledging that he had been the subject of our snooping—by any stretch. "I didn't talk to anyone at all. I just assumed it because you get to use the Map Division. We saw you there."

"Honestly, sir, we won't tell anyone about this,"

Liza said. "We're just kids. Nobody takes us seriously."

The part about not reporting this to anyone when we got out of here was Liza's first fiblet. Kudos to her for that breakthrough, I thought. The second part was all truth.

"Then why were you chasing me on Tuesday?" he asked, getting a bit too close to Liza for my comfort. "What do you think I did?"

"That was just a game," I said, trying to direct the heat back at me. "It was rude of us, I know."

"Since you like games so much, I've got an adventure for you," Savage said, stepping aside again. "Down the steps, girls. Immediately."

I thought of the number of times I had rudely defied my mother during my childhood. "You can't make me do that," I said, just as I had unsuccessfully said it to her so often.

"That's where you're quite wrong, miss," he said. "Get a move on before I push you."

I stood fast. I didn't budge until I saw the flash of a thin silver blade in Preston Savage's hand. And then I gasped.

Liza reached across and pinched my arm. Savage was holding an X-ACTO knife, with a precision blade, like the kind my art teacher used to cut thick paper when we did crafts at school. It must have been the metal instrument that dropped on the floor and caught Liza's attention on Tuesday afternoon, when Savage sliced a page out of a library book.

I didn't wait for the blade to get any closer to my face. I put my foot down one step and started to descend the broad staircase. Liza stayed at my side.

"There's no need to hurt us," Liza said. "We're harmless."

"I'll be the judge of that," he said, a step or two above us. "I just need to store you somewhere for safekeeping while I finish my work."

How did he think he was going to get back through that door, or did he have a fallback exit we couldn't see? Perhaps he knew his way around all the nooks and crannies of these old libraries. Maybe he had stored his treasures in forgotten stairwells like this one.

Twelve steps down and we turned a corner, down again, another dozen. There were no books to be found anywhere within sight.

Preston Savage circled around so that he stood in front of us. He took the phone from my hand and pointed the beam at an object on the wall above his head.

It was another sign that once had probably been electrified. It, too, said EXIT.

"But where are the stacks?" Liza asked, sounding as though she was about to burst into tears. "You can leave us right here and we can count to a million or something and not come out till late tonight."

"I think you two girls are a bit too curious to be left with a pile of books," Savage said. "And you'll remember that curiosity killed the cat, won't you?"

I heard the word "kill" and a chill ran down my spine.

"So I've got a better place for you," he said, pulling back the gigantic bolts that secured the steel door at its top and bottom.

While he wrestled with the old door, which seemed not to have been opened since the Dark Ages, I tried to think of all the advice my mother had given me. *Never get in a car with a stranger without putting up a fight, but on the other hand, don't struggle with someone armed with a weapon that could be used against you. Kick hard and run, or submit rather than be injured.* The choices were dizzying.

The door opened and the next space was pitch-black. "Give me your phone, too, young lady," Savage said to Liza, grabbing it from her hand. "You won't need it where you're going. There's bound to be light for you at the end of the tunnel."

Liza groped for my shirt and caught onto it. Preston Savage laughed like a madman, then pushed us through the doorframe and slammed it behind us. You didn't need Atwell ears to hear the dead bolts slide into place.

29

"A ghost station, Liza," I said, stepping out of the doorway, sliding to my side, and pressing my back against the blackened wall. "This is a ghost station."

"What's that?" she asked. Her voice was heavy, as though she was ready to explode with tears. "No one will ever find us here."

"We have to stay calm. If we cry, we'll never be able to see our way out, okay?"

"Wha—what's a ghost station, Dev?"

I stood perfectly still, taking in the sounds and the smells. I knew my eyes would need a few minutes to adjust to the dark.

The space had a terrible odor, dank and moist, like an old, abandoned basement that had been without light or sunshine for so many years. I didn't want to breathe the air in through my nose, afraid that it would make me sick to my stomach. I swallowed hard, but it was like gulping down something toxic that would burn my mouth and throat.

"Can you see yet, Liza?"

She lifted her arm to wipe her eyes. "It's too blurry."

The silence all around us was eerie, like we had traveled far below the surface of the earth where nothing else was alive. Every now and then I heard a very distant rumble—probably a train—that seemed always to be going in a direction away from us. Then it was quiet again, like a grave must be.

"I'm beginning to see shapes now," I said. My eyes were getting used to the pitch blackness of our underground cell. Below me, and several feet ahead, the railroad tracks that must have once gleamed shined dimly in welcome contrast to the darkness that covered both of us like a heavy blanket.

Liza stepped forward and I grabbed her arm to pull her back against the wall. "That's a subway track right in front of you. You've got to stay close to me."

I was ready to cry, too. But Liza needed me right now, so I tried to channel everything I had learned from Sam Cody about ghost stations. One of us had to stay strong.

"Remember, Liza, that first time we took the subway down to the Puzzle Palace?" It had only been Tuesday, but now it seemed like weeks ago.

"Yeah."

"I told you not to read on the train. I told you that you needed to keep your eyes open all the time 'cause a lot of stuff goes down, right?"

"I remember. I thought your subway rules were stupid."

My eyes continued to adjust to the interior of the darkened tunnel that stretched out on both sides of us. I could see the bright graffiti on the far wall, across the tracks—big letters and numbers in neon colors that had been sprayed on over the years.

"Well, maybe some of them are, Liza. But some actually make sense," I said. "Can you see those painted words yet?"

She picked her head up and stared straight ahead. "So what?"

"Think of it, Liza. Someone got inside here to do that—lots of kids—and that means they also got out of here. You just have to think about how happy my mom is going to be to see us at the end of the day, and that positive thought will help us work our way out of here."

"What does that have to do with subway rules, Dev?"

"I told you I always keep my eyes open on the train—no reading, no studying maps. That's how I learned about all the abandoned stations that were built," I said. "You can see some of them when trains pass by, even though they don't stop at any of them. Sam even walked me through one."

"Really? Is that why you're not scared right now?"

I hadn't said I wasn't scared. I just knew there had to be an exit from this horrible space and that we had to stay together to get out of it safely. I tried to breathe through my mouth and not my nose. The dust particles burned and made me cough, but the smells were much more sickening.

"There's an entire station right below City Hall, Liza—practically just across the street from police headquarters. One of the most beautiful places in Manhattan, but it's a ghost town. Sam got permission to walk my mother and me through it once, about a year ago. It's totally spooky, but having been there will help me get us back to the street."

"I'm not moving from this spot," she said, kind of plastering herself in place, sniffling a bit.

"But we have to walk, Liza. Nobody knows where

we are," I said. I didn't want to choke on the fumes that drifted through the damp tunnel and swirled around us. I didn't want to stay in a place where no one would be able to find us. "We have to try to search for a way out."

"These are subway tracks right below us. What if a train—?"

"They've been abandoned long ago, I'm sure. There's no sign or anything to mark this location," I said. "No benches, no lights. There's not even a shred of garbage around here. It can't be a real place."

"Why would the city abandon a train station?"

"It happened sometimes," I said, trying to dig for the stories that Sam had told me, while I clutched at Liza's hand. "There are almost five hundred subway stations in this city, and sometimes, when they were built too close to each other, one of them became obsolete."

"What are you doing, Dev? This is so dangerous."

My eyes were stinging now. It seemed that with each step we took I was kicking up scraps of broken tiles and mechanical debris that had been untouched for decades. If I rubbed my eyes, I knew I risked embedding the particles and making it impossible to see again.

"We're on the platform above the tracks. It's a perfectly safe place to be. We're going to walk single file, and I'll be in front. You just stay close to me. I'm going to pick a direction to walk in—starting off to the right—and you're going to stay as near to me as you can. Are you okay with that?"

"Was Preston telling the truth?" she asked. "Can you see any light ahead of you?"

I didn't want to tell her that seeing light at the end of the tunnel was just an expression. I couldn't make out anything more than what was five feet ahead of me. I had no idea if I was leading Liza to a dead end, or to a way out.

"Not yet, Liza. But I've only taken three steps."

The tunnel had a foul smell—a mix of old rusted metal and the fumes of the spray paint that covered the walls and ceiling. Aside from the distant rumble of trains, the only other sound I heard was the occasional scratching noise of nails against the tracks below. I knew it was caused by rodents larger than gerbils—now I could smell their presence, too. As long as Liza didn't ask about it, I wouldn't tell.

We must have taken thirty steps along the dusty platform. Liza grabbed the back of my shirt to steady herself. I looked at the stone pillar ahead of me and saw it had been tagged by several different artists. WHOIZTHEWIZ? stood out in cobalt blue, MIKEYGOLDLUV was painted in canary yellow, and WALLYDEGRAWDEMAN was bright red.

My courage was flagging. All I could think of was my mother and how devastated she would be if anything happened to me. I fought back tears of my own, realizing how wrong I'd been to disobey her.

Suddenly there was a huge gust of wind coming from in front of me. I stepped back, nailing Liza on her foot. She tried to balance us both and keep us on the platform as I jostled her.

I grabbed onto the giant pillar, passing on the side of it, and when I reached for the tunnel wall with my right hand, it seemed to start to curve. I was becoming disoriented by the change.

Then a screeching whistle—a terrifying burst of sound in the dead-quiet space—pierced the silent tunnel. The glaring headlights of a subway train meant that it was barreling down the tracks, coming directly at us and blinding me as it threatened to kill us, just like Liza had predicted. I closed my eyes, clenched my teeth to stop them from chattering, and flattened myself against the wall.

30

"You can open your eyes and stand up now, Liza," I said. I reached for her and helped her to her feet.

"I—I thought it was going to hit us," she said. "What happened?"

"I thought so, too. But it's a great thing, Liza. That proves this is a ghost station," I said. "There must be a place very close by, up ahead beyond this curve, where the tracks divide. The train just looked like it was coming this way, but the real station must be the one where we got off in Grand Army Plaza."

"I'm afraid to keep walking."

"You have to do it, Liza. Keep close and follow me."

It took a few minutes for me to collect myself and move forward. My knees were weak, and I wanted my footing to be more secure. I squeezed the imagined odors of dead rats and visions of giant insects out of my brain and urged us on. If I gave in to my fears—the moist chill of this underground cave, the blackness that was all around us, the thought that I would never see my mother again—I knew that we would lose our chance to get out of here.

Ten feet farther on and I could see it. "There *is* light, Liza! It's not the end of the tunnel, but there's a bright glare a quarter of a mile away."

"Really, Dev?"

"I promise you."

Liza was coughing, too. "Let's stop. I need to rub my eyes so I can see better."

"I don't want to stop until we get right there. And you can't rub this dust into your eyes. You'll never see anything."

I grabbed Liza's hand and pressed it between mine. "You're doing fine. Just stay right with me."

We stumbled along until we reached that point on the platform. I could see that it was a space where the curved wall ended at the very spot where the track made the turn into the actual subway station. The brightness was from narrow gratings in the sidewalk above the train tracks.

"Go there!" Liza shouted, almost pushing me in that direction.

"We can't do that," I said. "It's way too risky. The tracks are electrified and we have no idea how much space there is between the trains and the tunnel walls along that stretch."

"But can you see the real platform?" Liza asked. "Can you see any people?"

"Nope. We're too far from that. We've got to stay in the ghost station. It's a much safer place to be."

"What if we stand under that grating and shout up to the street. Won't somebody hear us?"

"You stand under that grating," I said, "and the next number three train that comes along will turn us into pancakes."

I stayed on the ledge of the platform on which we'd started our walk. The open space to the active tracks was behind us now. The tunnel grew darker again, and I had to readjust my eyes for the second time.

Despite the heat of the day, it was wet and cold in this subterranean space. Dank, dim, and deserted.

"What do you think you're going to find, Dev?"

"It's what we're going to find, Liza. You and me together, okay? There are always emergency exits in subway tunnels, Liza. All of them were built that way," I said, trying to convince myself that fact was not an urban myth. "In case trains got stuck between stations, there had to be ways to evacuate passengers."

"Have you ever needed to be evacuated?" she asked.

"Does now count?"

"I would have preferred that you've had a dress rehearsal, Dev."

"Hold on," I said. I could feel the steel railing before I saw it. "There's a staircase over my right shoulder."

I pivoted and could see that there were six steps leading up to a landing. The handrail was painted orange, and there was the muted glare of a stainless-steel box mounted on the wall.

I ran up the steps and felt around the edge of the box for an opening, but it was secured by a padlock.

"What does it say?" Liza asked. "Is it a phone?"

"No such luck. SIGNAL EMERGENCY POWER INLET is what the sign reads."

I ran my hands along the wall next to the box, feeling the grime accumulate on my fingertips as I followed the pipe that led away from the box.

"More steps above us," I said to Liza. "That can only be a good thing."

Orange paint bordered the ten steps that led farther up, which were so covered in graffiti that I figured the artists had been able to have easy access to this stairwell.

"What's at the top?" Liza asked.

"A ladder," I said. "An iron ladder with about six rungs. We're in business, Liza de Lucena, but you're going to have to help me here."

She was right at my heels, but I couldn't reach the lowest rung of the ladder.

"Cup your hands, Liza. I need a boost."

She stood beside me, leaned over, and held steady while I put my right foot into her hands and let her lift me up eight or ten inches. I grabbed the bar and swung loose for a few seconds, until I could pull myself up and stand on the bottom rung.

I climbed three more rungs until my head bumped against the ceiling above us. I held on with my left hand and reached up with my right.

I could feel an indentation in the steel design of the beams. I put my fingers on it and followed it around. There was a circular object cut into the heavy metal.

"We've got our escape hatch, Liza," I shouted.

My voice echoed through the tunnel. I wasn't worried about Preston Savage hearing us. He must have known where his own escape route was long before he trapped us in here.

"Can you see out, Dev?"

"Not yet. But it's a manhole cover," I said. "It means the street is directly above us."

"Move it, Dev," she was practically shrieking. "Hurry it up, will you?"

"I'm trying my hardest, but it's really heavy. These covers weigh about as much as I do."

I ran my hand across the inner surface of the iron plate. In the middle of it, I felt something protruding and grasped it with my fingers.

"Here it is, Liza. It's a hook," I said. "That means there's a pole to pry it open with, here somewhere, probably hanging on the wall right nearby."

Liza dashed to the wall and began to search for it, all around the space and high above her head. "Got it, Dev!"

She removed the eighteen-inch pole from where it hung on the wall and handed it up to me. It took me three tries to catch the manhole cover hook with the end of it, but finally I did.

I wrapped my left arm through one of the higher rungs of the iron ladder and pushed the pole and cover as hard as I could.

Nothing moved.

I tried a second time with no greater success.

I bent my neck and climbed up another step, reared back with my right arm, and gave it my best shot.

The manhole cover lifted almost an inch and then instantly fell back in place with a clang that had the fury of a loud thunderclap.

"Oh, no, Dev," Liza said. "We'll never get out of here."

"Don't jinx me, girl," I said. "I've finally got a use for all this upper-arm strength from my swim exercises and racing. I can do this, I promise."

It took three more attempts before I could make the cover move. This time I had my left leg intertwined on the ladder and both arms on the pole.

The manhole cover seemed to groan as it lifted upward over my head, and with one huge shove of the thick metal pole to propel it, I shifted it onto its edge. It started to roll away out of my sight from the space it had opened above us—flooding the shaft with sunlight—and I could hear the sound of cars braking sharply and horns blowing madly in the street where it must have landed.

Liza and I had found our escape hatch.

31

Liza and I were sitting on the back—on top of the trunk—of a blue-and-white patrol car by the time Booker reached us twenty minutes later. The two really nice patrolmen who had lifted us out of the shaft had bought us each a soda and ice-cream cone. The first thing we did was ask them to text Booker and tell him where we were.

They were the cops who'd responded to the runaway manhole cover that had stopped traffic on Eastern Parkway. They were pretty surprised to look down and see two of us—me clinging to the ladder and Liza pacing in circles below me—waiting for help in the stairwell of the tunnel.

Liza jumped off the car faster than I did and went running to Booker, grabbing him around the waist, and pressing her head into his chest. She was exactly where I wanted to be at that moment, but there was only room for one of us.

"I was searching all over the basement for you two," Booker said. "Where'd you go?"

"Ever hear of a ghost station?" I asked, wiping my filthy hands on my jeans. "And how'd you know to come to the basement anyway?"

"Ghost stations don't exist," Booker said, breaking loose from Liza.

"Bet that, Booker D," I said.

"You texted me, didn't you? That's how I knew to head to the basement," Booker said, holding his phone out to me. "You said you had found Preston Savage."

"I thought texts didn't work in the library," I said. "Wait a minute. How long ago did that come through?"

It had taken Liza and me more than an hour to get ourselves out of the abandoned tunnel. Preston Savage—who had taken my phone from me—must have surfaced much earlier. It was his exit from the library that triggered the text to go off to Booker.

"Maybe forty-five minutes ago," Booker said. "I've

been looking for you guys, with the library security team, all over the basement. How'd you wind up here?"

"Tell you that in a minute," I said. I was completely energized again. "That must mean that Preston Savage got away. We have to send out an APB right now."

"What's an APB?" Liza asked.

"Cop talk, Liza. All points bulletin. We've got to find this man before he gets away," I said, turning to the police officers.

"Just chill, Dev," Booker said. "Done with that."

"What?"

"Preston Savage has been arrested," he said. "You two besties cornered the guy and nailed him in the act. The detectives took him out of here in handcuffs, Dev. They think you girls are superheroes."

"We cornered him?" I said. "He's the one who locked us in a stairwell that led down to an abandoned train station. I'd say he had the upper hand. We just had to find our way out of the ghost station."

"Dev," Booker said, shaking a finger at me. "Stop exaggerating. Although that's going to be the least of your troubles when your mother finds out about this—what do we label it?—this adventure."

I grabbed Booker's arm. "Will you call her for me? Does she know Liza and I are okay?"

"Let's just say she doesn't know yet that you weren't always okay. She's kind of tied up in saving the world, big-time," Booker said. "I wasn't going to face Aunt Blaine till I had you two back to business. I stayed in touch with my mother and all I told her was that we'd see her tonight in the park. If I didn't have you and Liza with me by then, I might as well just pull a Houdini on myself."

"I owe you for that one," I said.

"You sure do."

I suddenly remembered our third suspect. "What about Natasha's friend, Jack Williams? Was there any sign of him today?"

"I'm pretty sure he's a good guy, Dev," Booker said. "You're going to have to rethink your coincidence theory. Jack's proof of that. He just picked a bad day to go to the library."

"How did they get Preston Savage?" Liza asked. "That's much more important."

I was so wired up talking to Booker I didn't even notice a man approaching our group from the direction of the library.

"When I came out of the map exhibit, I had Walter Blodgett with me."

"You actually talked to him?" Liza asked. "Was he in on it with Savage?"

"Total opposite," Booker said. "We decided to come outside to talk and were on our way to a bench in the plaza. The minute I stepped out of the library, some alarm went off around the corner and then I got the text from you."

"That we were in the basement with Savage?"

"Yeah."

"That means he was out of the basement already, too, if my phone worked."

"I didn't know he had your phone—I just assumed it was you—so I ran back in and got security to go down to the basement with me."

"Backup," I said, nodding at him. "Good policing, Booker."

"Where was Walter Blodgett during this?" Liza asked.

"I'd like to answer that myself." The well-dressed man who'd been on his way down the sidewalk stepped into our circle and introduced himself. "I'm Walter Blodgett."

The frown on my face sent a signal to Booker. I was

still thinking of the punch that Blodgett had thrown, and our suspicions that he had been an accomplice to Savage.

"Lighten up, Dev," Booker said. "Mr. Blodgett's on our side."

"I can't begin to express my gratitude to each of you," Blodgett said. "To you, Liza, and to you, Devlin. Booker has already told me so much about you."

"You know Preston Savage?" Liza asked.

"Our professional world of rare maps and books is a very small one," Blodgett said. "I've been an acquaintance of Preston's for many years, and sadly, in the last two or three, I came to mistrust him."

Liza and I exchanged glances—practically smiles—for the first time in hours.

"Preston came into our world as an academic," Blodgett said, "as something of a scholar. I, on the other hand, am a businessman. When I first had suspicions that my colleague might have been stealing valuable pieces from time to time, I became quite unpopular in library circles."

"Why's that?" Liza asked.

"I had no proof, Liza," he said. "No one believed me."

"Been there," I said.

"So I remained quiet about my suspicions," Blodgett said, "until Preston and I crossed paths one night, at another library."

"The Champlain exhibit," Booker said, pointing at me. "Harvard Yard, Dev. All props to you."

"You punched Preston Savage!" I said, so happy to connect all the dots.

"Not my finest moment, Devlin."

"You rocked it, Mr. Blodgett."

"Resorting to violence? I don't think so," he said, "but I was desperate to stop him."

"What did he do?"

"That night at Harvard, Preston never showed his face at the exhibition that we were all there to see," Blodgett said. "But just as I was about to leave, I saw him coming out of a private room, tucking some piece of paper into his sleeve. I opened the door to the room he'd been in as he was walking out of the library, and an atlas was on the table. I carefully turned a few pages in the old book, and sure enough, two maps had been removed from it. The tears were quite obvious."

"What did you do?" Liza asked.

"I didn't dare tell a librarian and be scorned again,

so I left the building after him. I wanted to accuse him to his face," Blodgett said. "I got lucky because he had driven to Cambridge, and so he had stopped to put something in the trunk of his car. Probably the stolen maps."

"The clue in the Puzzle Palace," I said. "Preston Savage's parking ticket from that night in Harvard Yard."

"I called out his name, and he slammed the trunk to walk toward me," Blodgett said, pausing to get the details right. "I made my accusation, told him that I was going to call the police to open the trunk of his car, and that's when he took a swing at me."

"Did he hit you?" Liza asked.

"No, but he didn't miss by much," the man said, lowering his head and his voice. "So I punched Preston Savage. One time, but squarely on his nose."

"You mean he's the one who called the police?" Booker said.

"I did, just as I had promised to do," Blodgett said. "But when they arrived, it was Preston Savage who had the bloody nose."

"And he wouldn't let them open the trunk of his car," I said.

"Exactly. And since they viewed me as the violent attacker, they didn't believe it was necessary to get a search warrant."

"You were arrested," Liza said, "and Savage declined to press charges."

"Yes, he just wanted to get out of town with his stolen goods. I tried to tell the police what I thought had happened, but Savage was the gentleman scholar with the injury to his face, and I was the angry businessman. They didn't seem to understand the value of one missing page of a rare book."

"You've been after him for all this time," I said.

"That's why I'm so grateful to you young ladies," Blodgett said. "When Booker got your text, he excused himself and ran off to find security. I was standing on the library steps, figuring he'd only be gone a few minutes."

"What happened?" Liza asked.

"A moment or so before your text rang through, I heard an alarm go off. You know the kind? Like a bell that rings when you go through a fire door that isn't supposed to be opened."

"Where was it?" I said.

"Somewhere on the side of the library. I saw several uniformed cops come running, so I walked around to see what they were after," Blodgett said. "It was some kind of trapdoor that came out of the library basement."

"See, Liza?" I said. "I knew Savage only locked us underground because he had his own way to escape."

"Not such a good one as ours," she said with a grin.

"Not good at all," Blodgett said. "As Preston was climbing out of the space, the cops stopped to question him. He was giving them some sort of story about what had happened, and he had some papers rolled up, which he was holding in his hands. I interrupted the officers and told them the papers—if they were maps—were likely to have been stolen."

"What did Preston Savage do?" I asked.

"He protested to the police, of course. Called me a liar and some other unpleasant names, but unlike the situation at Harvard, this time the officers walked him back inside the library with me to see which one of us was telling the truth. The head of the map division found the book Savage had been studying in the carrel where he'd left it a bit earlier."

"Left it when he had to get rid of us," Liza said.

"What the three of you have been up to all week," Walter Blodgett said, "has been an enormous public service."

"We didn't set out to do that, sir," I said. "We were just trying to get someone to take what Liza saw seriously. We never expected that it would lead us into danger, or to anything like this."

"I can't begin to tell you how it will affect our ability—scholars, librarians, booksellers everywhere—to tell the history of the world, for generations to come, as it has been told for centuries, through books and atlases and the rarest of old charts."

Liza grabbed me in a bear hug and squeezed me hard.

"You and your friends, Devlin Quick, have done something my colleagues and I have not been able to do, despite all our wisdom and experience," Blodgett said. "You've captured a map thief."

32

One of the things I love most about my mother is that she has never been the kind of person to say "I told you so." I'm trying to learn from her example.

By the time Liza and I got home late Saturday afternoon, after a debriefing by the Major Case Squad detectives who'd been summoned to the Brooklyn Central Library, I was really running on empty.

The Major Case lieutenant had told Sam Cody about the events of the day, and Sam—who really gets that my mother and I are lifelines for each other—sat my mother down to give her the blow by blow of our brush with a very bad man. I didn't envy him that assignment.

Sam also convinced the guys that Liza and I did not have to accompany the Crime Scene Unit detectives back into the ghost station to photograph and process the platform and route to our escape hatch. Our path through the dusty remains of an abandoned subway tunnel should have been obvious to anyone, and I couldn't face having to go back down there.

I don't think I'd ever been hugged as tightly as my mother hugged me when we walked into the apartment. She did the same thing to Liza, too. She wanted to be sure we were unharmed and uninjured. She made us each drink a mug full of hot chocolate—despite the warmth of the day—because it was my favorite comfort food and she considered tea a remedy for the sick and the old.

There was no scolding and no second-guessing. Not a hint of an attitude.

"How mad are you really, Mom?" I asked when Liza went to take the first shower and I was alone with my mother.

"Not the least bit, Dev," she said. "I couldn't be more proud."

"But I didn't listen to you. Over and over again."

"Liza saw something wrong and you believed in her, Dev. You backed her up when even I had doubts," she said. "You and Liza and Booker were searching for the truth, and you actually found it. That's what justice is."

When Liza came back into the bedroom with her bathrobe on, smelling so much better than she had all afternoon, my mother sat her down on the bed and began brushing her hair—telling her the same things she had said to me and trying to restore Liza's sense of well-being.

I made the shower as hot as I could stand it and stood in it for at least ten minutes. I wanted every trace of the subway tunnel erased from my body, even though it would live in my brain for a very long time. I think I had spent all my courage in the dark confines of the ghost station earlier this afternoon.

Both Liza and I still voted to go to the park for the evening. I didn't want us to be alone with our thoughts, reliving the day.

We walked over in a posse—my mother, Sam, Natasha, Liza, and me—meeting up with the Dibbles at our usual spot, pretty close to the stage.

Once we spread our blankets, I planted myself right next to my mother. I wasn't very hungry, so I just nibbled at the food. When she was finished eating, I stretched out with my head in her lap, needing to be close to her and sort of coddled by her like I was still a kid.

Liza had Booker on one side of her and Sam on

the other. Pretty good seating arrangement if you ask me. We decided to stay on our blankets, picnic and relax, rather than take our seats in the amphitheater. Liza was subdued, too, but happier with her companion—and with her fate—than Juliet.

It wasn't the right night for a post-performance photo op with the stars. All I wanted to do was go home and get in bed. I held my mother's hand all the way back to the apartment and slept better knowing that she was just on the other side of my bedroom wall.

She was the first person I saw Sunday morning.

"Hey, Dev," my mother said, stroking my head. "It's ten o'clock."

I pulled the sheet up over my head. "I want to sleep in," I said.

"No can do."

I opened one eye. "It's my RDO, Mom. Every cop gets a regular day off."

"You'll have to pick another one," she said, tickling the middle of my stomach. "You get a delicious breakfast—my only specialty—but then we have to be in my office by noon."

I pulled the sheet up again. "Oh, no. We have to go through the story again?"

"Not exactly," she said, getting up to wake Liza, too. "Mayor Bloomfield wants to meet the three of you. How's that for a reason?"

I was out of bed in a flash.

I thought my Ditchley blazer and clean white cotton pants would be an appropriate outfit for my mayoral meet and greet. My mother helped Liza pick out something sharp to wear, too.

Sam showed up half an hour later, in time for my mother's somewhat overcooked eggs and bacon. But I wasn't going to complain about anything this morning.

I could hardly sit still in the SUV on the way downtown. All the cops at One PP seemed surprised to see my mother on a Sunday, but they were on high alert and told us the mayor had already arrived. The Dibbles showed up five minutes later.

"Do you know the mayor?" Liza asked as we rode up in the elevator?

"I don't *know him* know him. I met him at my mother's swearing-in," I said. "Things like that. He's a really good guy."

Mayor Bloomfield was sitting at Teddy Roosevelt's desk when we walked in. I guess it kind of fascinated everyone who visited.

"Congratulations to you, Devlin," he said, shaking my hand. "They ought to name a wing of the library after the three of you."

"No, thank you, sir," I said, wishing Lulu could be at my side, too, to hear me refuse a suggestion of that kind of honor. "I don't believe in any of that. We just did what all good citizens would."

"You must be Liza de Lucena," the mayor said.

"Yes, sir."

"We didn't give you a very gracious welcome to our city, Liza."

"I like it here a lot, actually. I've made two wonderful friends, and it's a very exciting place to be," she said.

"I know the commissioner has something to say to each of you, but first, Liza, I want to give you a key to the City of New York."

I slapped my hand over my mouth so I didn't burst out with something silly. What an amazing gesture. I thought Liza's braces would pop off because of the size of her smile and the extra high five from Booker.

"It was your vigilance at our great public library, Liza, and then your courage and perseverance all week—your fearlessness, really—that has helped put an end to the destruction of some of the greatest treasures left in the stewardship of our citizens. I am sure your family and all your countrymen and women are as proud of you and as grateful to you as we are," the mayor said.

Then Mayor Bloomfield opened a large wooden box, topped with the crest of the city and lined in blue velvet, and presented Liza with a giant-sized gold key.

"I'm pretty much overwhelmed," she said. "I'm only here today because Commissioner Quick was so generous to offer me a place in her home, and then Booker and Dev were in this adventure with me every step of the way. I owe everything to them."

"Cred to you, Liza. You saw the crime happen and you never backed down," Booker said. "And Dev, you're an awesome private eye. No question about it."

Liza was full-on blushing. I couldn't tell whether it was because of Booker or the mayor or the shiny gold key in her hands.

"Thank you so much, Mr. Mayor," she said.

He took her by the shoulders and kissed her on each cheek.

"Now my favorite police commissioner has some business of her own," Mayor Bloomfield said. "Blaine?"

My mother took a black suede pouch from Sam Cody. She carefully turned it over so its contents slipped out onto her desk.

This time I gasped. There were three gold and cobalt blue shields—smaller in size than the traditional detective badges—but identical in color and design.

"I can't do better than Mayor Bloomfield," my mother said, "but I do have something for each of you. In recognition of your skills of observation, deduction, and detection, with great respect for your bravery, and on behalf of your devoted colleagues of the NYPD, it is my privilege to award each of you the title of honorary detective."

I was so excited I didn't know how I could contain my enthusiasm.

"Please step forward, Liza de Lucena," my mother said.

Liza handed her gilded key to Natasha and moved closer to my mother, who pinned the miniature badge on the collar of Liza's blouse. "Your courage and fortitude are remarkable, young lady. And one word of advice, if I may? From this moment on, in case you didn't know it, you don't always have to take direction from Dev, okay?"

Something about that made everyone in the room laugh.

"Booker Dibble," my mother said, motioning him to step up.

"Glasses or no glasses?" he asked, nudging me as he passed by.

"No glasses," I said. "Just be yourself."

My mother read Booker the same citation she had spoken for Liza. "Thank you also, Booker, for keeping these young ladies—*my* young ladies—as far out of harm's way as it was possible for you to do. Your undercover performance at the library, I'm told, was first-rate."

"Thank you, Aunt Blaine. I've got to say you're the coolest police commissioner on the planet. I'll wear this proudly."

My mother pinned the badge on Booker's shirt.

"Devlin Quick," my mother said, beaming at me.

"Excuse me, Commissioner," Sam Cody said, moving in beside her. "I don't mean to be rude, but I made a promise to Devlin—right in your kitchen—on Tuesday night."

I threw back my head and giggled with delight. Sam remembered after all.

"You did?" my mother said.

"Absolutely. I told Devlin that if she caught the thief, I'd pin the gold shield on her myself," Sam said.

"Then the honor is all yours, Detective Cody."

"Thank you, Commissioner," he said. "This one's for you, Devlin Quick."

I took a few steps closer to Sam and lifted the collar of my Ditchley blazer, right over the school insignia.

Sam squinted to latch the pin of the badge in place. "Now I know you were eyeing the key to the city, Devlin. But in your case, this shield is much more suitable. You already have that kind of key—in the person of your mother. She's given you all the tools you need—your brains, your heart, your courage, and your gift for friendship."

My mother was biting her lip. I knew what that was about. We were both on emotional overload today.

"Thanks, Sam. My mom even opened the door to the Puzzle Palace for us," I said. "I know I'm a very lucky girl."

"You're going to be one fine detective," Sam said. "You're already a supersleuth. You deserve this badge, Devlin Quick. You're officially one of us now."

Turn the page for a glimpse of

Devlin Quick's next case!

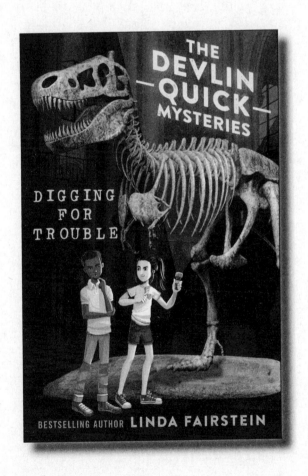

1

"I think I'm afraid to keep digging, Dev," Katie said.

We were both on our hands and knees, crawling up the side of a gulch in Montana, somewhere between the Great Plains and the Rocky Mountains. I turned over and sat up, reaching for a bottle of water from my backpack.

"You haven't got any reason to be afraid, Katie," I said. "Take a sip and chill out."

It was 94 degrees in the middle of the afternoon, and there was nothing—no trees, no bushes or shrubs—nothing to offer any shade to us as we inched forward over the brown sandstone surface of the hill.

"I don't want to be touching anybody's bones," Katie said, brushing off her hands. "That would really creep me out."

"It's not people we're looking for. It's fossils," I said. "Trust me, I'm not interested in coming face-to-face with human bones, either."

"Then why are you working so hard at this?"

I had a small hammer and a whisk broom, sort of a

handheld miniature version of a large sweeper, sticking out of my pants pockets. I had been using both of them—one to poke at rock formations and the other to brush away the dirt that covered them—as I made my way up the steep incline.

"C'mon, Katie. You like a good adventure as much as I do. There are supposed to be dinosaur fossils all over this valley," I said, sweeping my arm around in a semicircle, taking in the vast expanse of what the locals called Big Sky Country. "Isn't it cool to think we might find some of them?"

"Don't even mention the word 'cool,'" Katie said, holding the water bottle against her forehead. "I think I was six years old when my dad bought our ranch out here in Big Timber. I never figured Montana doesn't have an ocean anywhere around it. I really miss the beach right now."

"If you paid attention in science last year, you'd remember that where we're sitting this very moment was once the sea," I said, reaching over to fan my best friend with my whisk broom. "The Cretaceous Western Interior Seaway, right next to the coastal plains where gigantic dinosaurs roamed seventy million years ago."

"I can't believe that you actually did homework to prepare for this summer vacation trip," Katie said, rolling her eyes at me. "That is so Devlin Quick of you."

"I *am* Devlin Quick," I said, getting to my feet and giving Katie my hand to help her up. "Besides, your dad signed us up for this dino dig, and we've only got two more days to go. I'm getting fossil fever, for sure."

Katie Cion and I met in kindergarten. We were starting eighth grade at the Ditchley School in Manhattan—a private girls' school—after summer break. We were pretty much inseparable, and I was so happy her parents had invited me to spend two weeks at their ranch.

"Now what?" Katie asked.

"We've got a couple more hours to go," I said. "We have to reach that tent at the top of the ridge by five o'clock, for everyone to check in on the day's progress."

"Why isn't there a ski lift to get me up there, Dev? My legs are too short for this climb."

I was back on my hands and knees, trying to concentrate on unusual spots on the surface of the ground. "Think of it this way, Katie. Your very cute neighbor will be waiting at the peak, and I've seen the way you look at that cowboy."

"Kyle? You're ridiculous, Dev. He's just my Montana buddy," Katie said. "And he's fourteen years old. I mean, he's not interested in me."

Katie was back in position with her head just inches above the top layer of earth, probably so that I couldn't see her blush. She was pawing away at the dirt with renewed enthusiasm.

The land we were digging on was privately owned. It was a few miles away from Big Timber, which is the town where Katie's dad had built a ranch on the Boulder River. He liked to go fly-fishing, and the river that roared through the Cion's backyard was perfect for that.

"What do you think this is?" Katie asked, holding up a round gray object that looked like an ordinary rock.

"I have no idea. Why not wrap it in that soft material they gave us and put it in your backpack to show to Mr. Paulson?"

Steve Paulson was the man who was supervising the dig. He was a paleontologist—a scientist who studies fossils. The government doesn't fund much of this work, so Steve told Katie's dad that he liked to have volunteers to help him with summer digs.

About nine months ago, the rancher who lives on the land we were on today, found the giant leg bone of a dinosaur. He had just been out hiking on a path that went from his property into the state forest next to it when he spotted it.

Steve met with all the volunteers last night to explain

what we'd be doing and what we should look for. He told us he was pretty certain that the remote acres of land on the Double G Ranch were actually a bone bed—a dense deposit of fossil bones from prehistoric times.

Katie stopped and removed a length of light-brown padding from her pack. "This really smells gross," she said, wrapping the rock inside it and tucking it away.

"It's made from the hair of a camel," I said. "It's called camel matting. It's what they use in the desert to protect things they find there, like your piece of rock, because it's so soft."

"Cotton's soft, too, and it doesn't smell like it's been sweating in the desert sun for hundreds of years."

"Stop whining about everything, Katie," I said. "Get back to work."

Katie readjusted her hat. She was fair-skinned and blond, and needed to keep covered from the sun. I had black hair like my dad and a complexion that tanned easily, though both Katie and I had lathered up with sunscreen. Katie was petite and at least four inches shorter than me. I was what my grandmother liked to call a "gangly girl"—long-legged and lanky.

I scraped away loose dirt in hopes of finding buried treasure. Every now and then, I looked back over my shoulder to check out what the others were doing. Some were working by themselves, while others formed small clusters on the broad hillside.

I must have been ten or twelve feet ahead of Katie.

"Why are you going so fast?" she said to me. "I don't want you to leave me behind. Don't you know what the Double G stands for?"

"You mean the name of this ranch?" I asked. "Clue me in."

"My dad says the initials stand for Great Grizzlies, Dev. Like this land is totally covered in bears. That's what the place was named for."

I paused and looked back at Katie, laughing at her. "Not right here, that's for sure. Bears don't like the heat. They spend this part of the day sleeping in some shaded grassy spot. They're more likely to be under the cottonwood trees along the river in your backyard in Big Timber than where we are now."

I continued my climb up the slope, even though I was losing my patience. It was tough work to comb the ground for bits and pieces of stuff. I didn't realize how far I had gotten from Katie until I heard her shout my name out loud.

"Devlin!"

I stood up and glanced down at her, now thirty feet away.

"What is it?"

Katie's voice had carried across the hillside and almost everyone stopped in his or her tracks to look over at her.

I ran down, slipping as I neared my friend and landing on my tail. "What is it? Are you all right?"

"I'm fine. I'm perfectly fine."

There was a small bump protruding from the sandstone, covered in gnarled pebbles and sharp pieces of rock. Next to that were a few strips of gray-black stone that almost looked like fingers. Human fingers.

I let out a low whistle. "I bet they're dinosaur bones," I said. "They look exactly like the photographs Mr. Paulson showed us last night."

"The color is right," Katie said, almost shivering with excitement. "The size and shape are the same. They could be remains from small dinosaurs, couldn't they?"

Katie took a few more pieces of camel matting out of her pack and began to wrap the three pieces she had found. "This mat smells like perfume to me now."

I reached into my bag and pulled out the small can of orange-neon paint, spraying a large circle around the area to mark the spot of Katie's find, like Steve had taught us to do this morning.

Neither one of us heard the approach of the man until

he stood over us, the brim of his cowboy hat casting a shadow over my hand and the tip of his hiking boots practically stepping on the spray-painted marking I'd made.

"What have you got there, little lady?" he asked in a Montana drawl.

"Just some rocks, I think," Katie said, always fast-thinking on her feet. "I'm picking them up to give to Mr. Paulson when we get to the crest."

"Why don't you show them to me?" he said, holding out his hand to her.

"I don't know you, sir. I was told to hold everything until Mr. Paulson gets a chance to look at stuff first. I'm sure they're nothing at all."

The man crouched beside us. He was probably fifty or so. His skin was weathered and lined, and his out-stretched hand was bigger than a catcher's mitt.

"I'm Chip Donner. I work for Steve Paulson," he said, turning his eyes to me. "Nobody draws a neon circle on the ground around nothin', missy, do they? So why not just show me what you two found?"

Katie looked to me and I nodded. "Let him see, Katie. No harm in that."

She slowly unrolled her three little packages and set them back on the ground. Chip Donner glanced at the odd-looking pieces. He didn't crack a smile. I had no idea what he was thinking.

"Just rocks," he said. "You girls will learn soon enough. I thought maybe you had something real good, like a dinosaur tooth."

"We're pretty happy with these for right now," Katie said. "Whatever they are."

"Tell you what—Miss—?"

"Cion. Katie Cion."

"So you're David Cion's kid?" Donner said, reaching underneath the trio of camel mats with his huge hand and standing tall to hold them up over our heads, before I could get to my feet to challenge him. "Why don't I just help you out, for your daddy's sake? I'll walk these right up to the tent and make sure they get tagged and photographed and returned to you by the time you reach the top."

"We don't need help," I said. "Thanks very much but we're doing just fine."

"Wouldn't want you breaking up things in the event they have value," he said. "I wouldn't want you to get blamed for splitting these rocks in half in case you slip down again and fall on top of them."

"Katie's the most responsible girl I know," I said, but Donner was walking away from me faster than I could go, and Katie was still picking up her supplies from the ground.

"I can't believe I let that guy take off with my fossils, Dev," Katie said. She was close to tears and I understood exactly why.

"Cowgirls don't cry," I said. "The faster we can get to the top, the sooner we blow the whistle on him."

"But my bones," Katie said.

I grabbed her hand and started pulling her up the incline. "You didn't want any bones in the first place. Now get moving."

We reached the ridge about twenty minutes later, sweating and out of breath and completely disheartened.

The area under the small white open-sided tent held three tables, one of them set up with lemonade and cookies. The other two seemed to be work sites, where an assortment of specimens were laid out, each one of which was resting on a piece of paper on which the volunteer's name was written. I looked for three pieces the shape of Katie's find, but didn't see anything like them.

Two women were in charge of refreshments. Several of the older volunteers were seated on folding chairs, refreshing themselves, while others were chatting in small groups.

Kyle Lowry, Katie's Big Timber neighbor, was just getting off his dirt bike and ambling over to the tent.

"The worst thing happened to us just now, Kyle," Katie said.

"What's that?"

"Well, I found some things—Dev and I think they might be dinosaur fossils. And I guess I made too much noise, and the next thing I know this guy came down the hill and he took them away from me. Just snatched them and walked off."

"Steve Paulson?"

"No, Kyle," I said. "We met Steve last night. This man said his name is Chip Donner. He spooked both of us, to tell you the truth. Does he really work for Steve?"

"I mean the pieces I found aren't here on the table," Katie said, breaking in to my series of questions. "They're just gone."

"Don't get panicky, Katie," Kyle said, pulling his hands out of the pockets of his jeans. "They'll turn up. Donner's not a thief. My dad knows him from back home in Big Timber. Nobody working for Steve would be a thief."

"What do we do?" I asked. I felt sort of out of place here. Back in Manhattan, I was a lot surer of myself. "Should we ask Steve about this?"

"I don't think so," Katie said. "Not yet, anyway. I

don't want to bother him unless I'm really certain of everything."

"Whatever you think," I said. "I know who to go to for help when I'm at home, but this territory feels like being on a different planet."

"You're in the Badlands, Dev. The Montana Badlands," Kyle Lowry said. "Let's all just stick together. These parts didn't get that name for no reason."